I0676548

# Praise for
# Samantha Shu

## *Whispered Dreams*

"**Samantha Shu** brings an original and freely-imaginative approach to popular fiction that is refreshing. She comes out of a long and venerable line in British and American literature that includes such diverse antecedents as Edgar Allen Poe, Arthur Conan Doyle, Ambrose Bierce, Dashiell Hammett, Agatha Christie, Dorothy L. Sayers, and Raymond Chandler. Her writing particularly suggests Arthur Conan Doyle, in terms of its use of deductive reasoning and logic, and Dashiell Hammett, in its strong characters and narrative pacing. This latest work displays all the classic features of her unique approach, which blends hard-boiled investigation and relentless sleuthing with realistic dialogue and brilliant description. At a fundamental level, the novel explores a theme as old as the Bible – the conflict between good and evil – but the work transcends that conventional premise and brings us directly into the current, postmodern era, where people face existential decisions that define them as much as the provident or improvident actions they take.".............................John Murrray, (Colorado) author, *The Indian Peaks Wilderness Area: A Hunting & Field Guide*

~*~

"*Loved it!*.........." Kathy Lane (Texas) "Loved *Whispered Dreams*, didn't want to put it down. I can hardly wait for Shu's next one. I will be buying it as soon as it is released."

~*~

"*Awesome!*........." Sheryl A Brown (Parker, CO) "What a great read. Could not put it down. A must read for anyone who loves a good Romantic thriller."

~*~

"*Masterfully engineered!*........." Macelin Cane "Macelin" (Colorado) "Once again the words and rhythm of Samantha Shu have successfully tackled the art of a suspenseful thriller. From the very beginning, an intricate and mesmerizing tale of mystery and mayhem. As soon as you feel comfortably footed on solid ground, she sweeps you at the knees, leaving you gasping for more. Don't put it down - you won't be able be able to function in everyday life until you know........."

~*~

"*Thrilling!*.........." Jill K. Ross (Golden, CO) "What a thriller! Through every twist and turn, you won't be able to put it down. And who doesn't love a good heroine? Fantastic! A great read. Get this book! You'll love it."

~*~

"*Spine-tingling page turner!*.........." D. D. Morehead (Denver, CO) "A great read! Shu's characters are edgy and smart. Her dialogue is snappy and her plot complex and enjoyable. This book has it all for lovers of suspense, with a surprising ending that will shock you to the core. A must for your library!?

~*~

"*Supermom!*.........." Margaret J. Dolan, *Lover of Vamp Fiction* (Fort Worth, TX) "I loved this thriller! Samantha Shu is an excellent writer and *Whispered Dreams* is a fantastic achievement! Truly the right genre for her.

~*~

*"Truly outstanding!*........." Mid-Atlantic Book Reviewer "Samantha Shu takes her place among the top quality writers of suspense, romance and action."

~\*~

*"Top drawer entertainment!*........J. Jackson Owensby, *N.C. Writers Assoc.* (North Carolina) "Shu has produced a book that is impossible to put down. I did, and you will, read deep into the night as she keeps us on the edge until the last thrilling word."

# Blood
# Line

# Blood Line

By

## Samantha Shu

Argus Enterprises International, Inc.
North Carolina*****New Jersey

*Blood Line*
All rights reserved © 2009
Samantha Shu

No part of this book may be reproduced or transmitted in any form or by any means, graphic, electronic, or mechanical, including photocopying, recording, taping, or by any informational storage retrieval system without prior permission in writing from the publisher.

A-Argus Better Book Publishers, LLC

For information:
A-Argus Better Book Publishers, LLC
Post Office Box 914
Kernersville, North Carolina 27285
www.a-argusbooks.com

ISBN: 0-9841342-4-7
ISBN: 978-09841342-4-3

Book Cover designed by Sammy & Dub

Printed in the United States of America

# Dedication

I look into the future, realizing that I will only succeed in fulfilling my dreams by continuing to surround myself with fabulous people. As I have risen from a struggling writer into a published author, I have been supported by a group of generous, extraordinary souls.

  Thank you, Marjaree Mayne and William Connor, for allowing me to follow my dreams, while keeping me challenged and working with ever evolving markets in my field. I also want to thank John A. Murray for taking the time to share his expertise with a young writer. His work is amazing in a time when true literature is hard to find. John has also blessed this novel with a wonderful introduction, a gift I am truly grateful for. Ray Casperson, thanks for your invaluable first edits, as always. Thank you, Stormy, for being my inspiration. You are so talented for one so young.  And finally, in a sea of faces that have passed through my crazy life, my best friend has been my constant. Dub, thank you for the support you have always given without any need for reciprocation.

# Introduction

*I want to put a group of characters (perhaps a pair; perhaps even just one) in some sort of predicament and then watch them try to work themselves free...The situation comes first. The characters -- always flat and unfettered to begin with -- come next.*
..........Stephen King, from *On Writing* (2000)

As usual, Stephen King, the master raconteur of our time, said it best, when he spoke in his primer *On Writing* about the primacy of situation, which is another way of stating that circumstance precedes character and, for lack of a better word, destiny. The protagonist, of course, is the individual whose fate matters most to the reader. It is a characteristic of Samantha Shu's novels that the characters advance from a kind of nascent viewpoint to a deeper and deeper involvement in the ever-changing, ever-driving plot. The ability to chart that journey is the mark of a mature story-teller, and the growth or curve of the author's vision makes us all care about the development of the characters as well as the surface texture and the fine details.

*Blood Line* begins with a character in transition, as she finds herself in a new assignment and a new situation. The novel ends, forty-two chapters later, with a climatic and cathartic kiss. In between, we are introduced to, and subsequently follow, Charlie and

Devon and a host of other characters major and minor. Together they are engaged in a process of interaction and revelation. Like most literary works, **Blood Line** is concerned with a core set of truths. In a larger sense, as I have written of Samantha Shu's work elsewhere, the author is concerned here with a theme as old as the Old Testament, and that is the eternal battle between good and evil, darkness and light, and lawlessness and the law.

The first requirement of any work is what the novelist John Gardner called "*profluence*," which he defined as "*the sense that things are moving, getting somewhere, flowing forward.*" "*The common reader*," Gardner wrote, "*demands some reason to keep turning the pages.*" In the case of **Blood Line** we read simply because we find the characters compelling and the story immensely attractive. The dramatic tension is certainly there, as well as the intimate access to events that demand our attention. We turn. We read. We turn and read some more. Before we know it we are a third of the way through, and then half-way through. **Blood Line** is a page-turner, and the fact that it is -- at a time when many critics bemoan life in the "*post-literate age*" -- is a testimony to Samantha Shu's skill as a writer, and her deep knowledge of the human condition. Both are necessary to a successful novelist, and the absence of either has prevented many a work, however well conceived, from reaching its fullest expression.

All crime fiction, or detective fiction -- there are as many terms for it as there are critics -- go back to one work, and that is Edgar Allen Poe's 'The Murders in the Rue Morgue' (1840). Poe fathered the genre. He wrote the first detective story. In that seminal creation he established the form's main conventions, as well as separated it from other fiction genres, such as the science fiction story (Mary Shelley) and the fantasy story (Washington Irving). The first fictional detective, of course, was that presented by Arthur Conan Doyle. Sherlock Holmes (circa 1887) provided a primal model of brilliant sleuthing arising from keen powers of logic and observation. The genre reached its apex in the work of Dashiell Hammet, Mickey Spillane, Raymond Chandler, Agatha. Christie and hundreds of other fine 20th century authors. **Samantha Shu** stands out in this line, for her devotion to the female perspective, for her ability to re-imagine the world, and for the uniqueness of her 21st century *Weltanschauung.*

Long ago, in the forgotten afterword that he wrote for a trilogy of novellas, *(Different Seasons) that* later served as the basis for such brilliant films as *The Shawshank Redemption* (`Rita Hayworth and the *Shawshank Redemption*), which starred Morgan Freeman, and *Stand By Me* (`*The Body'*), which starred River Phoenix, Stephen King confided that the question he is most often asked by readers is "Where do you get your ideas?" One has the sense, in the case of **Samantha Shu**, that she takes her inspiration, first, from her own life, secondly, from the lives of those around her, and thirdly, from her own vivid and powerful imagination. She observes the flow of life and sees it all as a grand pageant struck through with light and dark. She knows that it requires commentators like herself in order to fully appreciate and understand. Once again, in ***Blood Line,*** she transcends expectation and takes us over the horizon, which is another way of saying she brings us back to the splendor and travail of this often troubled but endlessly fascinating world.

................John A. Murray 7-11-2009

# Prologue

Vision blackened at the edges, he asked himself, *'Why am I doing this?'* The answer seemed to be within reach but he couldn't quite seem to grasp it. The fog was overpowering him. *'Why am I holding a gun?'* A heavy mass of steel clenched in the hand of a villain, or was he a hero? Bewilderment; his grip so tight that his hand would carry the maker's trademark for hours.

The handle. Why was it so comfortable, the sensation like a hand-carved handle on an expensive British cane, but without the encumbrance of a three-foot extension? Was it actually lethal? Perhaps. However, in the hand of this individual, it was questionable. ...or was it?

...And then he saw her, standing alone, and he knew what he had come to do, what he must do. The only question was, *'Why?'* The fact that he didn't know did not seem to matter. His body was moving of its own accord. Walking toward her, he felt the ominous workings of this machine within himself fulfilling some command that he did not comprehend.

She was royalty, or so she thought, displaying the weight of a queen against the commonwealth seeming to surround her as she paraded through the open chamber of the castle courtyard.

Her act exuded more power than she had, for she was not the royalty that one would expect from the generations of upbringing that adorn the etiquette of such a lady. Perhaps this act, this pompous, arrogant, obnoxious act that he accused her of, was simply a force-fed illusion to better justify his forthcoming action.

Steeling himself to look at her, revealed finer detail than before. His eyes lost sight of everything before him save this woman, from head to toe a majestic sight, adorned in the crafts of many brilliant designers.

Her hair was gray with age but stylishly kept, the results of hours spent in an exotic salon in preparation for this moment. It was all so elegant. He studied her eyes; beautiful, blue and deep, echoing some remorseful past where basic essence was lost, an eternal sadness exposed.

Forgotten for a moment, the weight of the weapon returned, now even heavier than before, almost as if it alone was emulating the heaviness of the situation. The moment had approached like a stroke of lightning upon the scene. It was time.

He raised the gun as a highly trained marksman would prepare to gain true sight of his target, and without the hesitation expected of an amateur (which he obviously was not, though he did not remember engaging in training of any sort), pulled the trigger.

The two shots echoed off the walls of the courtyard and through the streets like the toll of the town's bell at a New Year's celebration. They were straight, true and accepted by their targets, not with pain, but the most powerful numbness...instant, sudden and completely effortless death.

The unfortunate demise of the two men accompanying the woman was not only a surprise to her, but to him as well, for until the gun exploded with the fire of a dragon's breath from its barrel-shaped mouth, he was sure that the target had been her.

Had he missed and struck these two innocent men who guarded the woman? Would a better aim or more time in preparation have prevented this mistake? He did not believe so. He had done what he had come to do.

This was the work neither of an amateur nor someone with even a great deal of experience, but that of a professional. This man (or beast?) who had pulled off this treacherous deed was not unaccustomed to death or its repercussions.

There was no pity or remorse, no pain felt, and beyond all that, no guilt. He had done his job and that was it. The end. No regret for the victims he had felled, for it was they who deserved this never-ending sentence to the afterlife.

Immediately following the hits came a return barrage of gunfire in his direction that caused his instant retreat into the shadows from where he had executed his attack. The bullets bounced and ricocheted off the walls of his alley of escape, the shooters in pursuit. Perhaps this phase had not been planned as well as his crime. How would he escape?

Nicholas Devon jerked awake, panting. Trying desperately to draw air into his tortured lungs, he could feel the sweat sliding down his chest. He raked his hands though his hair, climbed out of bed, grabbed a robe and headed downstairs to wait out another night.

# CHAPTER 1

Yesterday, her itinerary for the following four days had arrived. Packing, moving, airlines, and hotels had all been taken care of. Charlene Morgan looked at the letter attached to the itinerary and stared, still unbelieving, at the signature of the Acting Editor. Scrolled in bold letters was "N. Devon." Not for the first time, she hoped it wasn't the same N. Devon that she had so loved to hate in college. Because if it was, life was about to become anything but perfect.

As she drove to her destination she considered how lucky she was to have this opportunity. Two nights being pampered in a hotel had benefited her greatly. The paper was taking care of all of her needs just as promised. Having arrived at her new home yesterday, she was refreshed and ready for the settling-in process. Her furniture and personal belongings arrived on schedule and the movers had everything unloaded and in place within an hour. She was looking forward to taking this next step in her career.

It was only the morning after settling into her new home, yet Charlie was prepared for her 8:00 a.m. meeting at with the paper's editor-in-chief. Although she was ready in the obvious sense, her heart still hammered inside her chest and her palms were slick against the steering wheel. She tried unsuccessfully to convince herself that the reason for this had nothing to do with the signature she had been wondering about for the past few days.

Every scenario possible kept surfacing in her muddled brain, none of them were good. Her only hope at this point was that somehow there was another "Devon" with the first initial "N" that just happened to be a journalist. She was thinking that the possibilities of this were slim to none and that she was grasping at straws. She laughed at her musings, realizing that she was mixing her metaphors. She must be stressed. Charlie smiled to herself. The trick was to remember that she was no longer a twenty-one-year-old college student. She could handle anything he could throw at her, without getting angry or juvenile.

She pulled into a parking space and looked at her watch. The moment of truth had arrived; taking a deep breath she headed inside.

# CHAPTER 2

M ary inhaled deeply, leaned her head against the soft leather and tried to imagine she was heading toward something great instead of running from something horrible.

All memories of moments before this one were bright and hot. Her most fervent wish was that she could erase the reason for her present situation. Frequently on the move, hiding, thinking everyone was looking at her. She was darkly aware that her new course was based on a decision she was making to run instead of taking any kind of stand. The sorrow that filled her was sometimes so overpowering that tears would slip from her eyes unexpectedly and without consolation.

Even with her new hair color and her brown contacts in place she worried about being recognized. They were looking for her. There was a certainty, never felt before, that if they found her she would never again be given the chance for escape. She had known peace, love, and security. That was all over now. She ached with the knowledge that she would never again see her home, her family.

The name on her passport read, Mary Thomson. According to the details listed there she was 5' 7," 128 lbs., with brown hair and brown eyes. *'The new me'*, she thought with disgust. Mary listened as the plane readied itself for takeoff, wondering if she might get any sleep on the flight. As the plane started down the runway, Mary gripped the armrests and contemplated how she would proceed with the rest of her life.

# CHAPTER 3

*N*icholas Devon sat behind his desk and wondered fleetingly if this was a mistake. He immediately dismissed the thought and grinned, thinking how much fun this reunion was going to be. Life had been so mundane lately. All work and no play had made Nick feel like a very dull boy. But all that was about to change with the arrival of Charlene Morgan.

He remembered what a bitch she had been in college. According to her, nothing he had ever done was ever good enough. Starting school at twenty-five was a mark against him. Because of his age, he was much more focused than the younger students. Good study habits made it possible to keep up on his schoolwork as well as his responsibilities for the school paper. For some odd reason Charlie took his abilities as a personal affront and did everything in her power to make his life miserable.

On many occasions she had succeeded. This only served to make him work harder and eventually it became a game that neither person enjoyed playing, but both were addicted to. In his second year, he had left school to join the Marines and had always regretted his timing. When he had left, Charlie was winning the game.

Now eight years and many hard lessons later, Charlie Morgan's resume had crossed his desk. In spite of past history he never considered not hiring her. If memory served, she was fabulous at what she did. When he had last seen her she was at the top of her class and reveling in her success. She would be a valuable member of his team.

Admittedly, the real reason he had set the ball rolling almost immediately was his desire to finally put her in her place. He hadn't decided yet where that "place" would be, but he was sure he would make that decision in the next few hours. If her attitude hadn't changed in the last eight years it may not take that long.

His thoughts were interrupted by his secretary's voice as she peeked around the door; "Ms. Morgan has arrived."

He nodded, "Thank you, Betty. Wait five minutes and send her in."

"Yes, Sir," Betty replied and closed the door.

Nick spent the next five minutes deciding what story to start her off with. It would have to be something she'd have to work at making interesting. This would have to be an impossible mission, but one she couldn't say no to; a real challenge. Every good journalist hated boring stories and that was just what he intended to give her. Boring. He would make it very clear that he expected edge-of-the-seat editorial. He flipped through the pile of folders on his desk. Missing persons, deaths, abandoned animals; all stories put on the back burner.

"Perfect," he said, grabbing a folder from the pile. "Mary Fagon. Missing. Presumably having abandoned her husband and three young children." He read this aloud and smiled. If someone had been watching him at that moment, they may have been frightened. The smile was not pleasant.

The door opened slowly and Charlie walked into his office. When their eyes met, her pace slowed and her expression looked as if someone near and dear to her had died. Just as suddenly as he saw it, the look was gone.

She resumed her pace, all business again. Her control over her emotions didn't surprise him. In that way she hadn't changed; but in many other ways this wasn't the case. The unkempt college student was gone. A woman stunningly put together had taken her place. Nick stared. She had styled her hair in a tight French twist, although a few strands had escaped and fallen around her face. The color was the same deep auburn he remembered. Her make-up was subtle, just enough to accent her large pale gray eyes, full lips and high cheekbones.

She seemed taller than he remembered, somewhere near 5'9." Her deep green dress hugged her curves, accenting her small waist and flowing loosely around her legs. He wondered how it would feel to touch the skin now being caressed with each movement of her long legs. He caught himself before he groaned aloud.

"It's been a long time. You're looking well." He waved his hand motioning toward the chair opposite his. "Have a seat."

She took a seat, still looking a little stunned and said, "I must tell you, I'm a little confused by this situation."

Nick leaned back in his chair, put his feet on his desk, and said, "Please let me ease your confusion. What seems to be the problem?" He was really enjoying her discomfort. Yet, he was having a hard time remembering why he didn't like her.

"It's no secret," she began. "That we didn't have a wonderful working relationship, yet you hire me as a staff photographer with exciting journalistic opportunities and it's obvious you knew I was the same Charlene Morgan. So...what gives, Mr. Devon?" This last was said very sweetly.

"What gives? Well, let's see," he drawled, ignoring the "mister." and acting as if he didn't remember anything from the past.

"If my memory is accurate, you were and probably still are rather good. I can always use someone like you on my staff. As for our previous relationship, working or otherwise, was it really that bad?" he asked, all innocence.

A grunt was her only reply and it satisfied him immensely, letting him know she remembered him well.

"O.K. Point taken," he said. "The past is in the past; we're older and wiser now. I'm sure you'll do a wonderful job. Speaking of which, let's get down to business, shall we?"

Charlie looked at him skeptically, "You'll outline my responsibilities now?"

"That was the plan. Are you all settled and ready to get to work?" he asked.

Charlie was obviously having a problem assimilating the recent developments. "I assume I'll be sent out as staff photographer on all major stories."

"That is correct, as long as times aren't conflicting. In addition to your responsibilities in that area you will cover stories I assign you. You'll have the same chance of advancement as anyone. The only glass ceiling you'll encounter here will be one you build yourself." He paused looking at her, wondering what she was thinking.

Her face held no expression that could be deciphered as anything other than boredom. Knowing that boredom was the least likely feeling she was experiencing, he decided she had become much better at hiding her emotions. Bringing them to the surface would be fun.

"And," he said continuing, even as his expectations grew "I have a story that you can get your feet wet with."

Charlie sat up straighter and leaned forward slightly, "You're starting me off with a story?" she asked.

"Is that a problem? You said you were ready to get to work." For a fleeting moment he felt bad for her. She was so eager. He looked into her unusual eyes. Past memories of those eyes looking at him with scorn put him back on his earlier path. "Or did I misunderstand? Do you need more time?" he asked.

"Yes, no...I mean no I don't need more time. I assumed you'd start me with a photo assignment, since writing is going to be a secondary responsibility. Not that I have any problem with this. Actually, I'm thrilled. What's the story?" Her excitement was palpable

Nick grinned. It was beginning to scare him how happy it was to see her so disoriented. He would definitely have to get a handle on this before he regressed into juvenile delinquent status.

He looked at the file before him and said, "There's a missing woman.  Her name is Mary Fagon, maiden name, Thomson.  Husband Anthony Fagon reported her missing last Saturday evening.  Three children at home; two girls—seven and five—and one boy, six months.  There's a possibility that the disappearance is linked to postpartum depression.  The husband argues this point.  There are a few listings in the file of people to contact.  I'm sure you can take it from here."  He handed her the file and walked to the door.  "Come with me and I'll show you your desk."

Her "desk" was three doors down from his and sat in the center of a private office.  He could tell this surprised her and he was pleased.

"The dark room is on the second floor.  I'm sure you'll become proficient at negotiating the building soon.  In the meantime Billy, one of my runners, will show you around.  He'll be here at 10:00.  Until then, make yourself comfortable.  Any questions before I go?"

"Yes." Her voice stopped him. She didn't ask her question. She stood looking at him. Assessing him, he wondered what she was thinking.

When she asked her question, her voice was sweet, as if she were talking to a child, "Should I address you as Mr. Devon or would you prefer Nick?"

He looked at her standing there; tense, looking as if at any moment she might scream.  He wondered what she would do if he walked over, pulled the pins from her hair and tasted those full beautiful lips.  His palms began to sweat and he decided that wouldn't be the best beginning to their working relationship.  Still the thought was tempting.

"Just Devon, the mister sounds too 'old man' for my taste," he said.  There was a strange huskiness to his voice that he hoped she hadn't noticed.  Quickly retreating before he did something he would later regret, he headed back toward his office.  As he passed Betty's desk, he said over his shoulder,

"I'll be leaving for the rest of the day. Take care of things." He grabbed a stack of papers and left, hoping things wouldn't get out of control in his absence.

As he moved quickly out of the building he realized he might be taking on a dangerous task, playing with his new hire so blatantly. He considered the danger as he took the long way home, giving him ample time to contemplate this unexpected development. The extra time to think had done very little good. Today he experienced something he had imagined for years. It had not been at all what he expected. There was an added problem he hadn't considered.

Charlie was different. She was a beautiful, desirable woman. The desirable part was the problem. Nick wanted her, but knew he could never have her. Choices made in his past, left him with few options in his future. Nick had never been good at accepting the fact that he couldn't have what he wanted. Wanting Charlie was going to drive him crazy and he knew it. "I think I need a cold shower," he announced to himself. He hoped the water might clear his head.

# CHAPTER 4

Charlie was so angry; her body was shaking. That bastard was so transparent she had almost laughed in his face. Revenge. That was what all this was about. He wanted revenge for something that had happened years ago. She stomped around her newly acquired office voicing her anger in ways that would make most people cringe. When her tirade was over and felt in control again, she sat at her desk and thought about her problem, considering her options.

She could pack up and head back to Miami. Or, Option two: she could kill Nick and apply for his job. That was a good idea. *No, not Nick.* He had asked her to call him Devon. "Devon." She rolled it across her tongue. Yes, it definitely suited him better than Nick. It was darker somehow. Smiling to herself Charlie walked over to her desk and sat down. Her office chair was wonderfully comfortable. Turning in a slow circle she checked out her new space. This situation was unbelievable She remembered the start of it all. The past was creeping up on her.

Ω

Charlene Morgan, although she preferred Charlie, was born in a small town in Texas twenty-nine years ago. At age 18, she left and went to Dallas, where she worked her way through college waiting tables in the evenings and using her weekends to catch up on her studies.

In her sophomore year she became editor of the school paper. Her parents were very proud that year and bought her a new car. The car, a Toyota Celica, was the one expense that she had not been responsible for since high school and she treated it like gold. It lasted through-out the next four years, running like clockwork.

In her sophomore year of college, Charlie discovered a love for photography and it quickly became her minor, working wonderfully with her major, journalism. It was in this year that Nicholas Devon started working for the school paper.

Nick was the kind that never studied, partied all the time, and never had a problem making a deadline. His grades were always above average. He invariably had a beautiful girl hanging from his muscular arm. This wasn't surprising, because he was almost ridiculously gorgeous. His black hair was always a bit too long and mussed. She remembered his almond-shaped blue eyes and how she often thought they were just a shade too pale. Framed by brows and lashes the same rich shade as his hair, they were startling. He had a strong, square jaw that had a ten-dency to clench just under his ear when he was angry. The color of his skin was a deep, rich, natural tan, a gift from his mother's Native American heritage. He was also too tall, around 6'3", she thought. Everything about him was too something: he was too tall, too good-looking, too popular, and Charlie hated him!

Seeing how easy life was for Nick only made her hate him more. She would go out of her way to give him the most difficult stories, hoping he would fall on his face and even the playing field. The problem was he would always do a fabulous job. This only made things worse.

Sometime during her junior year, Charlie realized that he was aware that she didn't like him. She could see he was going out of his way to antagonize her. That year she changed her strategy. Charlie stopped giving him the more challenging stories and started doing them herself, spending hours that she didn't have to research and de-velop the best theories possible. She also kept up her grades and continued to edit the paper, doing as well as before. At the end of the year she was more tired than she had ever been, but the tables had turned. Now Nick

hated her and she had taken on his condescending attitude. Life was first-rate.

After spending that summer at home enjoying the
time with her very supportive parents, she returned to
school to discover that Nicholas Devon had joined the
Marines and left college. The competitive edge was gone
and Charlie was surprised by her disappointment.

Her senior year was not good. A close friend had
graduated the previous year and moved to California,
practically putting an end to what little social life she had.
The paper didn't have the same thrill it had before,
though she refused to admit to herself the reasons for
that. Topping it all off, she wasn't making great money
waiting tables anymore and the constant worry over tui-
tion was taking its toll. But despite all this, somehow, she
made it through and in the spring of 1998, graduated with
a major in journalism, and a minor in photography.

For the next seven years, Charlie lived in Miami,
working for the 'Herald', bouncing between staff photography positions, investigating leads for other reporters
and occasionally writing some inane article about the local
retirement community. A year ago, Charlie decided she
had gotten all she was going to get from Miami, which
now consisted of ridding herself of a southern accent,
acquiring a great tan and hitting a brick wall where her job
was concerned. She had to finally face the fact that in that
venue, her career had stalled. It was time to move on.

It took a year of sending out resumes and her port-
folio before she received a reply that caught her attention.
A paper in Denver needed a staff photographer with the
ability to occasionally report the news. The salary was
three times her current one and the possibility of a full-
time reporting assignment was available. She had responded and was granted an interview. The representative
for the paper was a genuine pleasure, the phone interview
went well and the job was hers if she wanted it. Yes, she
had wanted it! Finally! Ten years after starting college,

Charlie was beginning what very well could be the job of her life.

Ω

She pulled herself from her reverie and began perusing the file she had been given. It didn't take long for Charlie to realize that the first thing to do was contact the immediate family. She picked up the phone and dialed the number listed as Mr. and Mrs. Fagon. It rang five times before she decided to give up and try later. She was replacing the receiver when she heard a voice.

She quickly put the phone back to her ear.

"Hello?" she asked.

"Yes. Can I help you?" It was a man's voice. He sounded frazzled. Judging from the background noise it wasn't hard to figure out why. It sounded as if he were running a day care.

"Yes," Charlie responded," I hope you can help me. My name is Charlene Morgan and I'm with The Post. Am I speaking to Mr. Fagon?"

"Yes."

"I was calling to see if we could discuss a little about what happened involving your wife's disappearance?"

"Oh." With that simple utterance, his sadness was painfully apparent.

She tried to reassure him in soothing tones. "Mister Fagon, sometimes these stories can help. Someone that knows something might read it and come forward. I know this is hard for you but the most important issue here is to bring Mrs. Fagon home to her children." She paused there for effect. "And, to you." Charlie stopped and waited for his response, hoping she hadn't laid it on too thick.

"Do you really think a story in the paper would help? I don't want my kids bothered by the media. This is horrible for them and I don't want to make it worse."

She could only imagine the frustration he must be feeling. "Yes, Mr. Fagon," she assured him. "I think it will help. I'll come alone. No photographer and we'll just talk about what happened. I won't use the children's names in the story. How does that sound?"

Charlie could feel the indecision, it was almost palpable, but there was nothing left to say now. The decision had to be his. She waited. She waited and several seconds passed before he finally said, "Well, O.K., Miss Morgan. It feels wrong, talking to a reporter. I hope I don't regret it, but O.K."

Charlie hadn't realized that she was holding her breath until she felt the wonderful sensation of oxygen filling her deprived lungs. She tried not to sound too happy as she copied down the correct address and made an appointment for the following day.

# CHAPTER 5

Charlie arrived at the Fagon residence twenty minutes early. She hadn't been sure of the neighborhood and had given herself extra time to find it. It had paid off. Now she would have time to look around a little.

She sat across the street from the house and observed the lawn, wondering when it had been mowed last. The house was a ranch style, lime-green with hunter-green trim; very pretty. Toys littered the too-long grass. A black Range Rover sat in the drive. Everything seemed normal, no outward signs that mommy had disappeared.

Charlie left her car parked across the street and walked toward the truck. She peered into the side window. More toys, a car seat, again, nothing out of the ordinary.

She did not know what she was expecting, but this hadn't been it. When a family member was missing it seemed as if the grass should not be so green. The toys scattered around should not look as if they were recently played with. Nevertheless, the grass was very green and no weeds had grown around the toys anchoring them to the ground. Life was going on. The family was functioning despite their loss.

She knocked on the door and waited. Anthony Fagon answered the door and quickly motioned her inside. He then turned and headed for the back of the house. He said something that Charlie didn't catch. Then he yelled,

"Girls! Get in here!" It was obvious that he was not angry. His yelling was only to get the attention of the two little girls that came barreling into the room screaming,

"Daddy! Can we go outside?" Both girls were yelling as one, but in different order, canceling out each other's words. Despite this chaos, their father understood perfectly and said,

"After you introduce yourselves properly and calm down, then you can go outside."

The smaller of the two stepped forward. She looked up at Charlie with big dark eyes and smiled,

"Hi," she said, sounding as if speech was a rather new concept to the tiny child. "My name is Beka and I think you're beautiful." She pushed her dark hair out of her eyes. "I'm going to be beautiful too. My daddy says so." she said matter-of-factly. Her babyish voice only made her words more adorable.

Charlie bent down and took her small hand,

"Hello, Beka. Thank you. And I think you're very beautiful now."

Beka looked very pleased as she ran at full speed around Charlie heading for the front door. It was obvious she didn't want to waste any more time talking to adults when playing was on her mind.

The older girl stepped forward; she looked to be about 6 or 7. She was as light as her sister was dark. Her hair was almost white, her eyes blue. Charlie hadn't seen a picture of the missing woman, but she guessed that this girl looked like her mother. She held no resemblance to the dark-complexioned man standing behind her. His carbon copy had just run out the door. The girl held out her hand. Charlie could tell she was trying hard to be dignified.

"I'm Tallon. Are you going to look for my mommy? My little brother misses her. He cries a lot."

Charlie smiled at the sad, appealing little girl. "My name is Charlie and I write stories. I'm going to write a story about what happened and I hope it will help to bring her home. O.K?"

"O.K," Tallon said. She looked at her father expectantly.

"Sweetheart, go play with your sister," he said. Tallon brightened and started for the door. She paused and looked at Charlie.

"Can I read your story? I like to read."

"Sure. I'll bring you a copy," Charlie promised.

Tallon turned and went outside.

"She's taking it pretty hard. So is Kenny; that's the baby. Beka seems O.K. I'm not sure how long that will last. Wanna sit?" He motioned to the sofa.

Charlie sat as Anthony continued talking. "She's at that age, ya know. Everything is fantasies and baby dolls. It's good, I guess. I wish Tallon still had that attitude. She understands Mommy's gone and we don't know where she is. Beka probably thinks she went shopping. Kenny just knows she's not here. This is the first time Kenny hasn't had Mommy. She took him everywhere." He stopped talking and looked down at his hands. When he looked up, Charlie could see the unshed tears in his eyes.

"I'm sorry. I've been prone to babbling lately. Would you like some coffee?" he asked.

"Yes, that would be great," Charlie said, figuring it would give him time to pull himself together.

When he left, she looked around the living room. It had the appearance of professional decoration, paisley, hounds-tooth, and lace curtains. Everything decorated gorgeously. It was also surprisingly clean considering they had three children. Charlie wondered if they had a housekeeper.

Anthony returned looking in control again. He handed her a cup of coffee and took his seat. Charlie reached into her bag and pulled out a micro recorder and sat it on the table.

"When we start, I'll turn this on. It helps. This way we can just talk. I don't need to worry about notes and you can babble all you want. Is that O.K with you?"

Anthony smiled at her last statement. "That's fine," he said.

"Do you have a recent photo of your wife?" Charlie asked.

"Yeah, I do, but...I'd prefer you didn't use her picture in the paper."

"Of course," she said, "I'd like to see the photo for myself. It helps if I can picture who I'm writing about."

Anthony stood and left the room. He returned in less than a minute with a snapshot of a rather plain brunette, smiling, visibly happy. She was holding a small baby.

"That's the last picture taken; it was about a month ago."

Charlie looked at the snapshot; the woman looking back at her did not resemble Tallon's coloring, but the face was the same. The brown hair and eyes didn't seem to fit.

Odd, Charlie thought. Change the hair and eyes and the whole image changed. Where Tallon would grow into a stunning young lady, her mother appeared washed out and plain.

Charlie reached out and pressed a button on the recorder before she began the interview. "When was the last time you saw your wife?" she asked.

He answered, looking off into space, remembering. "Ten days ago. She was feeding the baby. I kissed her and she told me to have a good day. I went to work. When I came home, she was gone." His eyes came back, meeting hers. She was touched by the sadness there.

"Where were the kids?" Charlie asked.

"At the neighbors across the street. She called Mrs. Cain at three o'clock, asked if she could watch them. Said she'd be gone an hour or so."

"Did she tell Mrs. Cain where she was going?"

He nodded, "Yes. I asked her. She said Mary was going to meet a friend for a late lunch, but she wouldn't be gone long because she needed to get home to make dinner."

"Does Mrs. Cain normally baby-sit for you?" she asked.

"No. Only in emergency situations. We have a baby-sitter that comes to the house. But, she needs a little advance notice."

"Do you have any idea who Mary might have rushed off to meet?" Her question caused new tears to well up. She could see him trying to keep control over his emotions. It took a while before he could answer. Charlie waited.

When he finally answered, his voice faltered occasionally but otherwise he had gained control.

"Mary has lots of acquaintances, but no real friends. She's a very... private person. It's hard to get past the walls she's built. I've thought about that a dozen times and I can't imagine her rushing off at the last minute to meet anyone. Especially without Kenny. He very rarely left her sight." He paused and then added, "Until now."

Charlie knew that she didn't have a lot of time left before the interview would end. His emotions were very close to the surface. He wouldn't last much longer.

"Just a few more questions. In your opinion, would she ever abandon you and the kids?" She immediately felt the familiar guilt that comes from asking the hard questions.

"Never." Pain was visible on his face, but another emotion was there also.

She thought it might be fear, yet... she wasn't sure. "Was she happy with you? Were there any problems?" she prodded.

Anthony Fagon shifted in his seat and his answer did not match the fleeting emotions crossing his face. "No, we were very happy. We've always had a wonderful marriage."

Charlie knew he was hiding something. They were having problems; she was sure of it. She had identified one emotion clearly: guilt. He was feeling guilty about something.

She didn't feel he had done anything to Mary and he seemed genuinely miserable over the disappearance. However, he knew something that he felt was his fault. Whatever it was, he wasn't going to tell. She didn't push, trying instead to find someone else who may know.

"Can you give me some names of those acquaintances you mentioned earlier? And Mrs. Cain's phone number, if you have it handy?"

"Oh?" He looked confused. "Sure, but I thought you guys had the list of numbers. I gave it to that reporter yesterday."

"What reporter?" she snapped, then smiled at him, trying to cover her irritation.

"He said he was from the Post. He stopped by yesterday morning just after we spoke."

Now Charlie was confused. "Do you remember his name?" she asked.

"Mackenzie. Mike, I think. Yeah, that was it. Mike Mackenzie. He said he just needed the numbers. So I gave him a list. I want to help. I figure the more people out trying to get answers, the better. He is with your paper, isn't he?"

Charlie tried to hide her confusion. "I'm sure he is. I've only been with the Post a few days. I haven't been acquainted with all the reporters yet. He's probably just a runner. Can you give me the list anyway, just to be sure?"

"Yeah, it'll take a minute." He got up and left the room, leaving Charlie to wonder who in hell Mike Mackenzie was.

When she was assigned the story, she had been sure it would be simple. A woman runs off and leaves her family, short and sweet. Now things were getting interesting. She was certain that she was the only person on the paper handling this story. Devon certainly wouldn't assign something like this to more than one person. She was fairly certain that he didn't think this was very important. Especially if she was correct in her assumption that Nick

Devon was looking for a small measure of revenge. This was designed to teach her who was boss. Now someone was snooping around. Was it possible that Devon had misjudged and inadvertently given her a gift?

Anthony returned and handed Charlie a list of Mary's associates. He told her that they were written in order of importance. Charlie thanked him and asked, "If there are any other questions I'll need to follow-up on, would it be O.K to call again? I don't want to intrude." She tried not to let her solemn expression slip. She felt a thrill at the idea that something darker was happening here.

"Anytime. Anything I can do." He walked her to the door and held it open for her, completely unaware of her real state of mind. She walked slowly to the car and waved, contemplating the idea that 'Suzie homemaker' hadn't run away. '*Such a productive interview,*' she thought. A small laugh escaped her as she imagined Devon and his clenched jaw.

# CHAPTER 6

Charlie spent the rest of the afternoon calling the people on the list. The names that Mr. Fagon had given her seemed useless. They were neighbors, PTA members, and two women from a class in ceramics that Mary Fagon had taken two years before.

No one had called Mary the day of the disappearance; in fact, everyone Charlie talked with had told her they hadn't seen Mary in weeks. According to one of these women they had stayed in touch after the ceramics class and occasionally met to show off their current projects. The oddity of this was not lost on Charlie. This was a list of the closest people to Mary (according to the husband), yet it seemed she never had much contact with any of them.

Mary Fagon was hiding something from her husband or he was hiding something from Charlie. She was sure of it. Someone or something had been important enough for her to rush out without her children. Yet all of the closest people in her life knew nothing.

Charlie decided the next step would be to find out how Mr. Fagon made his living. She wondered if Mary had worked before the birth of her last child. If so, had she made any friends there?

She dialed the Fagon residence. After two rings a male voice answered. "Hello?"

"Mr. Fagon?" Charlie asked.

"Yes."

"This is Charlene Morgan from the Post. I'm sorry to bother you again. I have a few more questions."

"Anything I can do."

"Where are you currently employed?"

"Dealers Electrical Supply."

"How long have you been with the company?"

"It would be nine years now." he answered. He sounded tired.

"One more question and I'll let you go."

"Yeah?"

"Was your wife employed anytime during your marriage?" Charlie waited for him to answer. It seemed to take a little too long.

"No. She stayed home with the kids. That was important to her." His voice had taken on a tone she recognized from their earlier conversation and she knew he was lying.

"Thank you, Mr. Fagon."

"Sure," he said.

Charlie hung up. She began typing, what she had, in a neat, clean list on her computer. As she worked, her mind rambled through the details of her last phone call. It was peculiar that he would lie about Mary working. On one hand he seemed to desperately want to find her. He was prepared to have a reporter in his home, yet he would sabotage any help she may be. With a lie! *'Weird.'* What could he be hiding? Whatever it was, could it be important enough to risk her safety?

His employer, Dealers Electrical Supply; the name sounded familiar, Charlie couldn't remember where she had heard that name before. Maybe Mr. Fagon wasn't the sharpest knife in the drawer. Maybe he doesn't realize that talking to co-workers might shed some light on the situation. She shook her head; she was making stupid excuses, because she felt bad for him.

As Charlie contemplated her reaction, a tall broad-shouldered man with blonde hair and light eyes stood just inside Charlie's doorway. His back leaned against the jam while his legs stretched out in front of him. He played with a long cigar, rolling it between thumb and index finger, occasionally wetting it as if mulling over whether to enjoy it now or save the treat for some better-suited occasion.

Charlie, too distracted by her thoughts, did not immediately notice the man, giving him ample time to check her out, unencumbered by social niceties. Her face was rapt in total concentration as she typed, glancing occasionally to a small pile of papers to her left. A few loose strands of copper hair fell around her face, tickling the edges of her full mouth, causing her to brush them away or tuck them behind her ear. Invariably they fell forward again, irritating her. She reached up and pulled her hair back, securing it more tightly in a large silver barrette. While doing this, her head came up, her eyes meeting his.

"Well, hello there. I hope I'm not interrupting," he said smoothly, knowing that's exactly what he was doing

"No. That's fine," she said casually. She finished securing her straying hair and placed her hands under her chin, fingers entwined. "How can I help you?"

His posture straightened. He placed his cigar in a front shirt pocket and smiled widely, venturing closer.

"Just come by to introduce myself and let you know the lay of the land. "

"And?" she said, wanting to get back to her work. She needed to concentrate. This interruption was unwanted and she had no qualms about letting him see her annoyance.

"And?" he echoed.

She sighed, feeling the wasted seconds ticking by. "You said you came by to introduce yourself. Seeing that you have yet to do that, I have no way of knowing who you are. Would you like to get on with it?"

"Garrett Quinlan, at your service," he said smugly.

Charlie moaned. She had just been a total and complete smart-ass to the head writer. This did not bode well for her future on the paper.

"Excuse my rudeness, Mr. Quinlan. I am working on a story that has turned out a little meatier than I was led to believe. I'm Charlene Morgan."

He seemed a little taken aback. "You're writing a story? I was under the impression that you were our new staff photographer."

"That's correct. I was hired as staff photographer with secondary responsibilities as writer when stories are not front-page headline material."

"Ah, that makes sense. I guess I'll have to wait to use you then," he stated.

"Excuse me?" Her eyes snapped to his.

"As my photographer," he cleared up belatedly.

She had received this reaction before. Men in power positions often felt that by using subtle double entendre they could somehow set themselves above women. She'd risen above it in the past. There was no reason to change her strategy now. She swallowed her frustration and smiled at him, wide eyed.

"I'm sorry about that, Mr. Quinlan. Mr. Devon has assigned me to this story. He's as much as said this is top priority. If you need me to shoot anything for you, let me know. I'll try to fit it in."

For a fleeting moment, she was afraid she'd crossed some political line. Then his expression changed. he chuckled.

"I like you Charlene Morgan. We're going to get along just fine. My office is three doors down; just yell if you need anything."

"Thanks," she said relieved. She'd heard all about Garrett Quinlan. He was the best writer in Denver and everyone, including himself, knew it. The last thing she needed to do was get on his bad side.

He turned to leave. "Sorry we got off on such a rocky start," he said over his shoulder as he left.

Her train of thought was completely shattered. She looked at her notes and decided to go get coffee. She needed to clear the cobwebs. At the end of the first floor hallway, a large room was used for staff gatherings. Two extended card tables sat at its center. Along one wall, a counter top complete with sink and refrigerator were available for public use. The coffeepot was full. Charlie silently blessed the unknown soul who had made it.

She poured herself a cup and sat down in an art-deco chair that was lining one of the tables. She drank her coffee enjoying the solitude. It didn't last long. Within ten minutes, people she had never seen began filing into the room. She looked at her watch. 12:25pm. Lunchtime. She picked up her coffee and headed back to her office.

Charlie sat at the computer and spent the next two hours organizing and contemplating all the information she had discovered until now. It didn't add up to much.

There were lots of questions and very little answers. Tomorrow she would pay a visit to Dealers Electrical Supply. However, tonight she needed rest. "Time to call it a day," she said as she grabbed her briefcase and shoved her notes inside.

She left her office and wondered what Devon would say when he found out what a great story he'd laid in her lap. The thought made her laugh aloud; drawing looks from the people in the hall.

Ω

Charlie sat on her bed going over notes. She wore oversized T-shirt and red boxer shorts. Her hair was still wet from her shower earlier and she had piled it on top of her head and secured it with an oversized barrette.

The first week on the job had turned out to be more stressful than she had anticipated. First seeing Devon again and then that strange interview.

She looked around her bedroom. Boxes were stacked against the walls leaving just enough space to walk to the bed and the closet. Tomorrow she would begin unpacking.

Tonight she didn't have the energy. Sleep was what she needed. Unfortunately, it wasn't coming easily. She put her notes aside and went downstairs. On her way to the kitchen she stopped and put on a CD, "The Phantom of the Opera". In Charlie's opinion it was the best soundtrack ever made. The music serenaded her as she made a cup of hot chamomile tea and toasted a bagel.

On her way back upstairs, she grabbed a book out of the nearest box and looked at the cover: the latest novel by Stephen King. Perfect, something to take her away for a while.

Armed with her tools to acquire slumber, she went to her room and settled down for the night, enjoying the sounds of the music from downstairs. The book was typical Stephen King and took no time to suck her into its imaginary world. When she glanced at the clock on the nightstand sometime later she was shocked to learn that several hours had passed.

She stretched and yawned. Putting her book aside, she closed her eyes and quickly slipped into oblivion and soon was dreaming about Devon. He was sitting on his desk talking about how much he disliked the color blue. Charlie was sitting in a chair across the room.

She looked down and realized that she was dressed entirely in blue. She tried to lift her hands, they wouldn't budge, and then she saw the ropes. She was tied to the chair.

He moved to her and ran a finger along the line of her bottom lip. She shivered. He had never touched her before. He was so beautiful—no, that was wrong; not beautiful, sexy. She liked that his bottom lip was larger than the top. She didn't like that he appeared angry with her. His finger left her mouth and touched his own. The movement was incredibly erotic, and then he leaned in and said something she couldn't understand. Devon was speaking but not making any sense. His mouth was moving and yet nothing was coming out but gibberish. She realized he was ringing. The gibberish was a ringing noise. She kept thinking how she had to answer him but didn't know how.

Charlie's eyes slowly opened. Her telephone was ringing. She reached out and gripped the receiver pulling it to her ear. His voice was clear and strong. Before she could get beyond the sound of it and rise from her sleep-clouded space, she mumbled, "Why did you tie me to a chair?"

A sexy chuckle tickled her ear, his response rolled over her. "It's my lucky day; now I know what you fantasize about. Interesting." The last word was said slowly, as if he had just discovered something very appealing.

She was tired and could barely understand as he told her to have copy on his desk first thing in the morning. When she heard his end of the line go dead, she dropped the receiver and slipped back into slumber, this time unencumbered by distorted dreams.

# CHAPTER 7

Charlie remembered just enough of the night before to be mortified. She sat, waiting, just as she had all day. She continued trying unsuccessfully to get more work done. She knew at any moment Devon would walk through her office door with a grin on his face the size of the Grand Canyon.

She had placed a breakdown of her story on his desk. She knew it wasn't what he had expected. He'd given her an assignment that was very simple and, in his mind, it should have been completed by now. Instead of following his instructions she placed on his desk an outline for a much juicier story. He wasn't going to be happy. She only hoped he saw her copy before he came to see her. Anger was far more appealing than the arrogant attitude he was sure to have after what she said the night before.

She waited as long as she could stand it, and then decided he must be torturing her. She gathered up her notes, closed her laptop, and prepared to leave for the day. It was getting late anyway and she was starting to feel hunger setting in. It had been a lengthy day, and very little was accomplished.

So far Dealers Electrical Supply had been a bust. Anthony's boss was on vacation and his secretary was not authorized to give out any information. Charlie decided to go home and get some writing done. Walking down the hall she heard the telephone ringing in Devon's office. She paused and listened. It continued ringing.

# CHAPTER 8

*O*h great! Lost in a new city on a Friday night. 6275 North Wadsworth. That's the address the man gave on the telephone except that damn address doesn't exist! 6270 jumps directly to 6280, no 6275 anywhere.

*'Maybe I'm on South Wadsworth and don't realize it!'* Charlie thought, secretly blaming Devon for all of her problems tonight. Lately he was all she could think about. "What the hell is wrong with me?" Charlie said aloud, breaking the silence of the interior of the car.

Following leads was always the worst part of this job. Never having been in danger before it, had always been just a simple annoyance. Now, with an overriding fear, everything became so much worse. Normally with an article, she took the pictures and someone else wrote the story. This time it was different. Putting anyone else on this would also be putting him or her in danger. Therefore, for now anyway, Charlie was reporter and photographer all in one. Her earlier conversation that brought her here surfaced in her mind.

She remembered answering Devon's phone on impulse and had received a shock when a low voice said, "I have information about Mary Fagon. Go to a place called Dream World and ask for Tarrin. She'll tell you what you need to know. The address is 6275 N. Wadsworth. Go alone."

That had been all he said and now here she was in the middle of the night looking for some strange woman named Tarrin.

"Damn! There it is!" she exclaimed, pulling into the dark parking lot that occupied the space between 6270 and 6280. She saw the ordinary-looking building at the rear with the sign 'Dream World' on the door.

Stepping from her car, she had a hundred thoughts racing through her mind. She walked toward the door, preparing for the interview to come. Placing her hand on the door, she steadied herself. "Okay, here goes every-thing," she whispered.

Stepping through the door, Charlie stopped mid-stride and stared at a most unexpected scene. Three women sat on a couch in what looked to be someone's living room, dressed in next to nothing.

The room was very homey, complete with coffee ta-ble, television, and in one corner, a small area for making and storing food. The center of the room opened onto a long, narrow hall leading to a closed door. The color scheme was very rustic in coppers and forest green. The whole place seemed an incredible contradiction.

She realized she must have been staring open-mouthed, when a small blonde woman sitting in the mid-dle of the group, said rather loudly, "May we help you?"

Charlie shut her mouth and nodded, "Is there a per-son by the name of Tarrin here this evening?"

At this, the blonde looked to her left at a rather pret-ty redhead, smiled and said, (in that 'oh, isn't that interest-ing?' tone) "Well, that would be you. Wouldn't it?"

Tarrin stood, looking a little nervous. "Follow me," she said, "And we'll talk in the back."

As Charlie followed, the strangeness of the situation accosted her again; then finding herself in a small room complete with spinning lights and mirrors, being told to sit on the couch.

"I've been expecting you," was all Tarrin said, for a moment sitting down on what could only be described as a stage. She looked at Charlie as though she was an alien, "I told my ex to call, but I thought he'd be smart enough to get a man. Sometimes he's about as bright as a candle. You have fifty dollars?" she continued. "That's what it costs for a half an hour and it'll take that long to do this.

I thought it would be good to have you come in; do a show and no one would be the wiser. But now he's sent me a woman and I'm going to have a shit-load of questions to answer later, so let's make this look good." After finishing her speech, she laughed nervously and held out her hand.

'*Okay!*' Charlie thought. Now she was beginning to understand why the phone call had gone to Devon's desk. It was supposed to be a man. '*Awkward!*' She almost giggled as she reached into her purse to find the money. Charlie handed her the cash.

Tarrin said, "I'll be back in a minute."

She waited in the tiny room that resembled something from a '70's disco, and couldn't believe her luck. If she hadn't answered that call, she would have lost control of her story. The idea of Devon taking this from her was unacceptable. So here she was pretending to be a lesbian buying time with a pretty girl. Charlie was just beginning to get worried when the door opened and Tarrin came back in.

"Everything is taken care of. I told the other girls you were into fantasy conversation and we're going to talk for a while. And I'm really sorry for being so rude earlier, it's just this situation has me on edge." As she talked, she walked around the room turning down lights, fixing the radio, as if she'd done it all a million times.

"O.K," she said, sitting down across from Charlie. "Ask away."

Charlie didn't hesitate. "Tell me how you know Mary."

"I worked with her in a club about a year ago. She helped run the place. I guess you could say it was a family business. Really nice person. Good heart, and definitely didn't belong in this business. She was the kind of girl that only did it out of some sense of responsibility to the family or something. Anyway, I started working with her and we hit it off."

"When was the last time you saw her?" Charlie asked.

"About six weeks ago. I went by her house to see the baby. She seemed real nervous, I asked why, but she didn't say much. Then when I was leaving I noticed Tony, that's her husband, standing outside. Just standing there, looking like he'd just seen a ghost. Really weird. He's a great guy normally, always says 'hi' asking about things, really sweet, you know?"

"Yeah, I know," Charlie acknowledged.

"Well, anyway that's why this seemed so strange. I said 'Hey, Tony' and he didn't say a word, didn't even look my way. Just stood there like he didn't see me. So, I got in my car and left."

"So Mary wasn't acting strange, just nervous?"

"Yeah, but from what I've heard from people around the business, she's gone. Just disappeared. Do you think Tony did something?" Tarrin began to wring her hands.

Charlie, considering this, asked, "Is that what you think?"

She shook her head emphatically "Oh...no! Tony was acting strange that day, but he loved Mary. I mean really loved her! I never saw them fight; he'd call in the middle of a shift just to say how much he loved her. That baby she had... wasn't even his." She paused there and waited.

Charlie was confused by the last statement. "That doesn't seem to be something that fits into your argument. Doesn't that in itself give him a motive to do something to Mary?"

"Oh, you don't understand," Tarrin said, smiling. "They had two children; little girls, real cute kids. Sweet, too. Anyway, he had a vasectomy after the last one and she came up pregnant. It turned out that she had been having an affair with this guy and apparently wasn't too careful. So she realized she screwed up real bad and confessed everything to Tony. He forgave her, and was there through the whole thing, and, man, he really loves that baby. They were the perfect couple." She stood and walked to the stereo. She turned it up a few decibels and continued, "Sometimes having something to work out can make a relationship better in the end. That's what happened here. I've never seen two people so comfortable with each other. So, no, I'd bet my life he wouldn't ever hurt her."

"Do you know the name of the man she was having the affair with?" Charlie asked, hopeful.

"No. Mary was pretty close-mouthed when she wanted to be. But I did get the impression that it was someone Tony knew. Don't ask me why I think that, 'cause I haven't got a clue." She smiled, looking pleased with herself, and for a moment Charlie wondered if all of what she'd said was true.

"Well, if there's anything else you remember, please give me a call. Thank you for your time." Charlie said, handed Tarrin her card and left, feeling sure that there would be another telephone call from this woman. She definitely knew more than she was saying.

# CHAPTER 9

When Charlie walked into her office the next morning, Nick Devon was sitting in her chair with his feet on her desk.

"So," he said. "How was your meeting?"

"Great, thanks. May I ask why you're sitting at my desk? Is yours under construction? If that's the case, they're doing a marvelous job of keeping the mess out of the hall."

He chuckled, "Still quick as ever. No, my office is fine. Thanks for asking. I'm here to find out if you've made any progress on your new story. I was surprised to read the outline. Very interesting, Morgan. So, as it turns out, your first story is looking meaty."

Devon stood up, his boots hitting the floor with a loud crack that snapped Charlie out of her state of shock. She had been sure he would be furious that things hadn't gone his way. Instead he looked calm. He even looked happy. This was not at all what she had expected.

Charlie snapped her mouth shut and watched with trepidation as he came closer.

He was wearing cowboy boots and jeans and walked with incredible assurance. It poured from him, from his almost too broad shoulders to his narrow waist and long legs. She couldn't believe he still looked this good. She knew she was staring but couldn't seem to stop. His white shirt stretched across his chest and gloriously flat stomach. Her eyes kept moving down and she was vaguely aware that this was a very bad way to be looking at your boss.

"See anything you like?" he asked.

Her eyes snapped up to his. There was laughter there. She wanted to laugh, too; at herself, for being so juvenile. Her hormones hadn't run amuck this badly since...well; it was the last time she had seen HIM!

It angered her that he could rile her so easily. "Yes," she said, "I find you beautiful. You've kept in great shape over the years and your coloring is still as striking as always, although I do like the way you wear your hair now. Shorter suits you better." She gave him the biggest most innocent smile she could conjure up.

He threw his head back and laughed. It was a deep, contagious belly laugh. Soon they were both laughing and the tension had eased; they looked at one another and smiled.

Devon spoke first, "Have a seat and let's talk."

"O.K." She walked around her desk and sat down. He took the other chair and leaned back, looking relieved.

"I've been going over your report and it looks good. I wasn't expecting a big story."

"I know, Devon but..."

He cut her off, "Stop expecting the worst, Morgan." He stood up and started for the door, "I like what you're doing. Keep it up. If you need anything, let me know. O.K.?"

She was floored, very happily floored. "O.K., Sir."

He stopped and turned around, facing her, "Wow! Sir? Did I just earn a little of your respect?"

"Maybe just a little. But don't let it go to your head."

"Oh, you have nothing to worry about there. You have years of ego crushing to make up for. I want that copy on my desk in five days." He paused before walking out the door, "Hey, Morgan?"

"Yes?" she asked with trepidation.

"If you ever feel the need to have me tie you up, all you have to do is ask." The last of his words ended on a chuckle.

Charlie moaned and threw a pen at his head. He quickly ducked as the pen slammed against the closing door and fell to the floor, never completing its mission. Charlie laid her head down on the desk and took three deep breaths. She was mortified.

When she lifted her head she was staring directly into Garrett Quinlans' eyes. He smiled, handing her the failed projectile.

"Lose something?" he asked.

Charlie moaned. She didn't think she could handle two pompous men in the same hour. She held out her hand taking the pen.

"Thanks," she said grudgingly.

Garrett brazenly sauntered over and sat on the edge of her desk. He leaned in and smiled. "Is Devon giving you a hard time?"

"If you only knew." Charlie countered.

"Give him a chance. He grows on you."

The last thing that Charlie needed growing on her was Nicholas Devon. "Did you come in here for a reason?" she asked.

"I noticed you work late hours. So do I. Just wanted to let ya know if ya need anything after hours, I'm your man."

"Thanks, that might come in handy. Lately, I've had to leave when Angie leaves. I haven't been here long enough to rate a key."

Garrett smiled smugly, "Well, I have and I'm happy to share."

He stood up. "Just came by to say hey and offer assistance. You seem to be butting heads with the boss. That's never fun."

After he left, Charlie decided she liked Garrett Quinlan. He had delusions of grandeur, but a good heart.

Ω

The rest of the afternoon passed by quickly. Charlie called everyone on the list, checking and re-checking all possible leads.

Now that she had the go-ahead, the stress had diminished drastically. She had put in a call to Carl Vail at Dealers Electrical Supply. After calling the company to do a little digging, it wasn't hard to discover whom she needed to speak to and Carl Vail was the guy. She needed some background on Anthony Fagon's work habits. Did he work overly long hours? Did he have problems with co-workers? She needed these questions answered.

Carl Vail hadn't been in, so Charlie left a message for him to call her. She let his secretary know that it was important that he receive the message this evening. She had hoped he would call before she went home.

She was at the end of the hall when her phone rang. The machine picked up just as she reached it. Charlie could hear her own voice announcing that she was out of the office. As she picked up the handset, she said "Hold on, please," hoping whoever was on the other end would not hang up. The machine's electronic tone went off. Charlie pressed the 'off' button on the machine and said, "Charlene Morgan's office; can I help you?"

The voice at the other end of the line came on, "Hello, this is Carl Vail. I was told that you were trying to get in touch with me."

"Yes, Mr. Vail. I'm writing a story about the disappearance of a Mrs. Fagon. I was hoping that you could give me some information about one of your employees, Anthony Fagon, her husband."

"I thought that might be why you were calling. Tony called me yesterday and asked me to help you in any way I could. So, Miss Morgan, what is it you would like to know?"

Charlie was pleasantly surprised. She hadn't expected Anthony Fagon to promote her story this strongly. "I was hoping you could let me look at his personnel file. Would that be a problem?"

"No, not at all. I'm going to be at my downtown office until ten this evening. Would you have any time tonight?"

She jumped at the opportunity to do this quickly. "Sure! Can you give me directions?" She jotted down the information he gave her and hung up. She looked at her watch. It was 6:15. That would give her just enough time to get there by seven. Before the front door was in view, Charlie was aware that it was raining. She could hear it pounding on the roof. She was not looking forward to getting wet.

# CHAPTER 10

etting wet in the Colorado rain was a sure way to freeze yourself into a strain of influenza. This rain was nothing like the rain in Florida. There it was warm and soft. You had to love it or learn to because it rained every day, usually around 3 o'clock. And if you didn't love it, then there was a definite downside to living in the 'Sunshine State'. Derived from her love of this all-seasonal experience, driving in the rain had become one of her favorite things. If it weren't for the destination this would be a relaxing diversion. The rain was torrential and seemed to be mimicking the rhythm of the music on the radio. That, in conjunction with the windshield wipers, created a pleasing symphony.

Charlie sighed wistfully and began looking for the street where she'd been told to park. She recognized the gas station on the corner as the one given in the directions. Charlie pulled over, grabbed her duster, took a deep breath, opened the door, and stepped directly in the center of a puddle the size of Lake Michigan.

"Son-of-a-bitch!" she gasped, slamming the door. "This is getting better and better." She took off in the direction of the address, jogging at first and then realizing the futility.

It had only taken the first few blocks to soak her through to the skin. Slowing down to a fast walk, she began plotting her strategy. The point here was to pick up the paperwork and act like that was the only purpose. Slip in a question here and there; find out if Mary had spilled anything about her past. Easy enough.

'*O.K, second building after the sixth block on the west side of the street. This is it*'. The front door was locked, of course. She'd been warned this might happen if she arrived late.

The rain was making this seem less and less worth the trouble. The cold was seeping into her muscles and making them ache.

She turned and started making her way to the side of the building. There was light coming from somewhere. She couldn't tell the location; the rain dripping into her eyes, obscuring her vision.

Charlie moved toward the light hoping it was coming from the building's side door. The wind whipped her hair in front of her face. She didn't see the fallen trashcan until it slammed against her shins. Pain permeated her body, sending shock waves directly to her brain. Falling to the ground, she groaned.

"Shit! Shit! This is so not worth this! Shit!" She sat there in the alley for what seemed like an hour but was actually about 60 seconds, before she realized the light was coming out from a crack under a door to her right.

Her only thought at this point was getting out of the rain and into the warmth of any interior. *If this is the wrong door, I'll find the right door after I've dried off a little'*, she thought.

Grabbing the handle she pushed it open a crack, pleasantly surprised that it was unlocked.

"Well, at least something's going right," her voice sounding hoarse to her ears.

Preparing to step into what had become in Charlie's mind a sanctuary, she paused listening. A voice raised to the point of screaming was coming from inside. Some instinct told Charlie this was not a typical argument. Something dangerous was happening inside. Everything inside told her to go. Leave now. She continued peering through the crack in the door, trying to identify where the voice was coming from.

A freestanding lamp, beside a love seat against the far wall, gave light to the room. Off to the left was a hall leading to several doors. *'Offices'*, Charlie assumed. The room was deserted. She stepped through the door, closing it behind her. As an afterthought, she turned the knob making sure it hadn't locked in case a fast getaway was needed. She started down the hall. The voice was getting closer; she could hear part of the conversation. The tone was male and angry.

The door at the end of the hall opened and Charlie ducked into the nearest office, hoping she hadn't been heard above the yelling. She left the door open just enough to see as two men passed by. From her position, crouched behind the door, she only saw their backs as they passed.

The man in front was short, maybe 5'7", give or take an inch. He had blonde hair and very well could be the person she was here to meet. The other man towered over him and was wearing a hat, making it hard to tell his hair color. Something about this man seemed familiar. She was about to make a connection when the first man screamed,

"I told you I have no idea what you're talking about. Please, don't do this." There was real fear in his voice. He half turned.

Charlie glimpsed his face before the other man shoved him and said in a calm voice, "Sit down, shut up and listen."

He had a strong English accent and sounded like undiluted evil. The man, whom Charlie now realized from his voice, was indeed Mr. Vail, turned and sat down on the love seat, looking extremely uncomfortable. The larger man, still with his back to Charlie, leaned over and brandished a gun in Vail's face. He was frightening and commanding. Charlie felt sick with fear from the scene before her. A million questions were raging inside, warring for supremacy. She tried to quite them by focusing on the man with the gun.

"Open your mouth" he said in the same dead calm tone. Vail opened his mouth and a tear slid down his cheek. The other man, the Devil, in Charlie's opinion, placed the barrel of the gun in his mouth, "O.K.," he said, "Now we can discuss this like gentlemen."

Charlie's heart was pounding so hard she was amazed it wasn't audible to anyone but her. The Devil continued speaking and it took all of her concentration to hear above the pounding in her ears.

"Some very important people have informed me that you are a nasty man. The kind that takes information from someone who cares about you and then uses it against them. That's low. Don't you agree? No, don't try to answer, just nod your head if you agree."

With difficulty because of the gun barrel in his mouth, Vail slowly nodded his head. Charlie could clearly see the tears rolling freely now. His eyes were wide and she thought if he hadn't wet himself yet, he might soon.

"Good," the Devil said, "Now we're working on a good rapport; keep it up and you might come out of this bloody mess with your life." Again, Vail nodded slowly.

"Fabulous. I'm going to tell you a few things I would like you to tell me. Don't try to speak now. There'll be plenty of time for that when I'm done. Number one, I would like you to tell me about the young lady you were dating without her husband's knowledge.

"Number two, I would like for you to inform me of her whereabouts.

"And, number three, or lastly if you prefer, I want you to give me reasons why I should not end your miserable little life.

"Now this last I want you to make very convincing. The reason for this is that, I want to kill you. I find you useless. I personally don't see any reason to let you live. But I'm always willing to listen. Do you understand what I'm telling you?"

Again Vail nodded, this time closing his eyes.

"O.K. I'm going to remove the gun now and I advise you not to raise your voice. I deplore rudeness."

Charlie watched as the Devil slowly removed the gun from Vail's mouth, scraping it against his teeth. The sound seemed too loud. His mouth remained open for a second and then slowly shut. He looked down at the barrel of the gun and Charlie did the same noticing for the first time that it was equipped with a silencer.

"Oh shit!" Charlie realized too late that she had said the words aloud. Both men's head's snapped in her direction as she slammed the door and groped in the dark for a lock. Her hands found a small lock on the knob and turned it, knowing this would not stop him if he came after her.

Time slowed, her mind working furiously. "Who's here?" the Devil's voice called angrily.

"I...oh Jesus. What are you doing?" Vail screamed,

"I'm going to put you in hell. Tell me now who's here."

"I don't know. I don't...oh God please!" Vail's voice was shaking now, the words garbled, "Morgan, that reporter. Her...I...oh shit...Morgan, that's her name."

Charlie fell to her knees and crawled toward the back of the room, looking for something to use as a weapon. It was so dark in the room she couldn't see anything.

All her muscles ached as she felt for something to swing. She thought if she could find anything to swing at his head, she might buy some time, giving her a chance to get out past him.

If she could get outside and run she might have a chance. There was nothing. She groped in the dark feeling for anything. Not a simple desk or chair was available. A trashcan might do the job. But there was nothing. The room was empty. Every inch of space, empty. Now frantic, she stood and felt her way back to the door. Why hadn't the Devil come for her? She held her breath and listened.

They were talking. Vail sounded frantic, the other man sounded angry and she thought she detected fear in his voice. No, that couldn't be, she thought crazily. He wouldn't be afraid. She strained to hear more clearly.

"Morgan? There's a reporter here?" the Devil's voice raised, "Why? Don't answer that. It doesn't matter.

Stay put. I'm going to move to the door. I'm warning you if you move an inch I will end your puny existence."

Charlie knew this was it. She started thinking, racking her brain for ways to get out of this. Nothing. Nothing!

She stood leaning against the door wondering if this was how it would end. Just as she was deciding she would fight with everything she had, she heard a crash and what she would describe later as a "wet thump" and a loud voice cursing, "Bloody hell!" And then silence.

Charlie wondered for a second if she had become so frantic that she had blacked out. She pressed her ear to the door; still only silence. She slid down, sat on the floor and waited.

After a while, she began to realize she was alone. Her mind was working again. Opening the door didn't seem like a smart thing to do. She started speaking to herself in a whisper, "I'll wait a couple minutes and then I'll open the door."

Her voice sounded good to her, verifying the fact that she hadn't blacked out and that this may not be the end of her life. She counted the minutes, trying to prepare for the worst.

All possibilities needed to be considered. Something had happened on the other side of that door. Something bad. That was all she knew. The question was what? Was this owner of the Devil-voice, who had threatened to send Mr. Vail to hell, on the other side of the door, waiting? She hoped with what little energy she had left that he wasn't.

Time passed slowly. Seconds crawled by. She could hear nothing from beyond the door. When she couldn't stand it any longer, she stood, placed her hand on the knob and turned. The door opened and Charlie could see the light from the front room. The lamp had been knocked over and lay on its side, casting an eerie glow across the floor. Lying a foot or so in front of the door, face down in a puddle of what looked like chocolate syrup, was Mr. Vail.

Charlie ran. She moved as if there were no soreness now. With the agility of a gymnast, she jumped over the corpse, slammed her shoulder against the door and entered the alley at a dead run, her feet splashing in the puddles. Fear pushed her forward. Turning the corner she continued toward her car, never noticing the man leaning in the shadows watching, calculating his next move. She passed him and continued as though the devil himself were riding her heels.

After what seemed an eternity her car came into her field of vision. Breathing had become difficult. Her lungs burned, her vision blurred, but none of this mattered. She was alive and had every intention of remaining that way.

She slowed her pace and reached into her pocket, trying to locate her keys. If she didn't make it to the car the keys might make a good weapon. It seemed funny in a hysterical way that she hadn't thought of that earlier.

They weren't there!

Charlie reached the car shaking from more than the rain and cold. Frantically she searched every pocket. Nothing.

She pounded her fists against the hood of the car, then slid down, sitting on the curb. She had been sitting in this position for sometime before she noticed a car was coming.

She looked up and stared dumbly as a black Ford truck pulled in behind her. Nick Devon opened his door and jumped out. Relief flooded her. Tears slipped from her eyes and blended with the rain. She leaned against the car door and tried to stand. Failing, she slid to her knees, no longer having the power to hold herself erect.

"Charlie?" Devon said, he reached down and picked her up as if she weighed nothing. On the way to his truck he asked again, "Charlie? Can you tell me what happened?"

She looked at him and nodded not trusting herself to speak.

"Good," he said. "You're not in shock." He placed her in the passenger seat and ran around the truck. He slid in and pulled off his leather coat laying it over her legs. The truck was running and a wonderful heat hit Charlie and made her shiver convulsively.

Charlie took a deep breath and announced, "There's been a murder. You had better call the police. My fingerprints are all over the doors, my keys are there, and I sorta witnessed it." She leaned back and closed her eyes and was amazed that only silence followed her startling statement.

"Hello?" Devon said. Charlie opened her eyes expecting him to be speaking to her. He was holding a cellular phone. "Let me speak to Detective O'Brien, please," he continued, "Yes. Tell him it's Devon. Yes, I'll hold."

Looking at Charlie he gave her a reassuring smile and placed a hand over hers. "Terry?"

Charlie listened.

"Devon here. We have a problem. You may want to bring a team down to Parker and Fifteenth." A long pause. "Yeah. My staff photographer witnessed something here. A murder. Uh…" He looked at Charlie, "Do you have the exact address?"

"218 W. 16th, ground floor, side door on the east side." Charlie replied. Devon repeated the address on the phone.

"O.K." he said. "You got that? Great. I'm taking her home...no. No, my house. Two hours? O.K, we'll be waiting. Thanks! Bye." He pressed the disconnect button and turned to look at Charlie.

"I'm taking you to my house. No arguments out of you. Detective O'Brien is on his way. He's a friend of mine. He's coming by to get a statement in two hours. We should have you cleaned up and back to normal by then. You look like you could use some T.L.C."

Feeling bullied again but not having the energy this time to fight back, Charlie nodded and sighed audibly, before saying, "I suppose I'm at your mercy."

"Well isn't that a switch," he laughed, and started toward home.

# CHAPTER 11

Detective Terrence O'Brien was a burly man with white hair and blue eyes that seemed faded from too much use. Under normal circumstances he was quick to smile. This was not the case now.

He had been pacing in Devon's living room now for over an hour while Charlie went over her statement trying to remember every detail.

The interview was beginning to take its toll and Charlie was becoming irritable. The relaxing hot shower she had taken earlier was all but forgotten. She answered the same question she had been answering for the last twenty minutes. "I did not see his face. His back was facing me the entire time. He was wearing black. I couldn't begin to describe his build other than the fact that he was tall.

"He had on a trench coat and hat. I had a feeling he had dark hair. I can't explain that because I never saw it. Maybe his skin color. But I'm not sure. He seemed calm and professional until he realized I was there. That's when things went haywire. He lost it. I can't understand why he left me alive. That seems strange. He couldn't have known I didn't see his face." She paused, for a breath then said, "Oh, and he had a strong English accent." Charlie sat on the nearest sofa and looked up at Detective O'Brien. "But you already know all this. I'm just repeating myself now."

"All right, Ms. Morgan. Get some sleep. If I need more information I'll be in touch." O'Brien turned and glanced at Devon leaning against the wall, observing.

"As for you," he said, "Keep her out of this, no future involvement. Unless, of course," he switched the direction of his statement, directing this last at Charlie, "You would like to be implicated in this crime." He headed toward the door; she was not surprised that he'd had the last word.

# CHAPTER 12

When Charlie opened her eyes fresh panic set in. She had momentarily forgotten where she was. Then it all came back. Hiding in the office, the murder, being questioned...all of it. She closed her eyes and wished it hadn't happened. This tactic had never worked before but her philosophy was there's always a first time.

When she opened her eyes the second time, she was disappointed. The surroundings remained the same. Devon's bedroom. "Ugh," she groaned and reached up to massage her temples.

The smell of fresh coffee was coming from somewhere in the house and seemed to be calling her name. She pulled the covers aside and stretched like a cat. Feeling somewhat better, she slowly climbed out of bed, pulled on her jeans and grabbed a sweatshirt that was hanging on the back of a chair. That accomplished, she headed in the direction of the coffee.

Devon was sitting at the table reading the newspaper, sipping his coffee. He was wearing jeans, no shirt. Charlie stood at the kitchen door, taking in the sight of him. His skin was a deep golden brown. She knew that was from his Native American heritage and not from exposure to the sun. A small line of black hair started at his breastbone and disappeared in the waist of his jeans. His chest stomach and arms were covered in visible muscle. Lines of blue veins ran down each bicep accentuating his obvious athleticism.

She hadn't realized she was holding her breath until it escaped sounding like an explosion in her ears.

Devon's head snapped up. His eyes immediately made contact with hers. "Hi, sleepy head," he grinned knowingly. "Coffee?"

"Oh...ah...yeah, thanks," she stammered feeling her face go red. She hoped he wouldn't notice. No such luck.

"You look flushed. Are you sure something cooler wouldn't be better?"

"No!" she snapped. "Coffee's fine."

At this point she realized he knew she had been watching him. *'Caught in the act. There's nothing worse'*, she thought.

He handed her a cup. "There's cream on the counter if you need it."

She added cream to her coffee and settled into the chair across from him. "There are a few things I'm curious about," she said. "So I was thinking, maybe you would like to enlighten me."

"Mmm?" he hummed as he continued reading the paper.

"Why did you show up last night? Did you know I'd be there?"

Devon took his time folding the paper before he answered. "Yes. I knew where you were going."

"How?" she asked, suspicious.

"You left the machine on," he said matter-of-factly.

"What?" she sipped her coffee and looked at him over the rim, waiting for an answer.

He placed his paper on the table and looked at her with what seemed like frustration. "When you answered the phone, had the machine picked up?"

She thought about the telephone call. How she had been leaving the office when her telephone rang. How she had run back to get it in time and picked up after the machine.

She remembered saying "Hold on," and then the beep. Had she let it record the conversation? She didn't think so, but how else would he have known?

"Do you make it a practice of listening to my messages?" she said, dismissing the possibility that he was lying and moving on to the fact that he had invaded her privacy.

"No, Charlie, I don't make it a practice. However, lately you have been playing it just a bit fast and loose. I'm aware of this, so when I see you hightailing out of the office and your light on your machine is blinking, I take my chances.

"I couldn't believe you would go off halfcocked at night in that weather for paperwork on Tony Fagon. I knew there had to be more to it. So I went to find out. I suppose it was a good thing I did, wouldn't you say?" He gave her a genuinely innocent look that she had come to realize was bunk.

"Fine," she said. "I'll let that slide for now. But if you saw me leave and went out after me, why did it take you so much longer to arrive? I was there for quite some time."

He put his hands in the air as a sign of surrender. "No thanks are necessary." His voice dripped sarcasm. "The next time you're in danger, if I happen to show up a little late I'll just continue on my way."

"That's not what I meant and you know it. Why are you being evasive?" Now she was curious. It seemed odd the way he was avoiding her question.

He mumbled something under his breath and looked back down at the paper on the table.

"What was that?"

He looked up and she was surprised by the look of embarrassment on his face. "I got lost."

"Oh," She tried not to laugh and failed. By the time she regained control of herself tears were rolling down her cheeks and Devon's face was red.

"I...suppose..." residual giggles escaped her. "You would like to change the subject?"

"That's a good idea." His embarrassment had changed to annoyance.

"Fine. Oh, and by the way...thanks." She directed her brightest smile his way and stood, "Time to go to work. Can I use your shower?"

"Sure."

She didn't look at him as she left the room but it was obvious by his curt answer that this was not his happiest moment. She smiled, genuinely enjoying his discomfort. This just might turn out to be fun after all, she thought, as she headed toward the bathroom.

# CHAPTER 13

The chance to find out any information from Carl Vail was gone and Charlie was stumped. Why would someone kill the boss of a kidnapped woman's husband? It didn't make any sense. But that just added one more item to the long list of things about this story that didn't add up.

She looked down at her list.

#1. Mary missing, leaving three kids and husband.

#2. Tony Fagon, distraught, swears they were doing well.

#3. Someone acting as reporter snooping around.

#4. Carl Vail calls, ready to hand over records.

#5. Carl Vail murdered. Why?

Reading and rereading and hoping something would jump out at her. She leaned back in her chair and thought, I can't write a story about this, it makes no sense. "Shit!" The frustration was obvious in her voice.

The phone rang. She picked up before the second ring. "Charlie Morgan."

"Hello, Ms. Morgan. Detective O'Brien here. I would like to speak to you today. Are you free for lunch?"

Charlie was surprised by the strange invitation. She sat up in her chair intrigued, "Yes, I'm free."

"Great. Do you know O'Malley's?" he asked.

"Yeah, I know it" she said aware of the sports bar and its tendency to be empty till happy hour rolled around.

"Great, I'll meet you at O'Malley's. Is 11 o'clock good?" he asked.

She was quick to respond "Sure. Yeah, I'll see you at 11 o'clock."

"Great, great. Bye." The line went dead. Charlie held the phone, looked at it as if it were an object she didn't recognize, and said, "I didn't think my life could get any stranger."

Ω

O'Malley's was slow, but housed the usual lunch crowd. Charlie found Detective Terrence O'Brien sitting in the back in a booth, smoking a cigarette and taking large gulps of something that looked suspiciously like an alcoholic beverage.

He looked up as Charlie arrived at the table and smiled. It didn't reach his eyes. "Ms. Morgan. I'm glad you could meet me on such short notice."

Charlie sat down across from him and wondered if he was on duty. "Well, I must tell you, your phone call took me by surprise," she said, hoping to get to the point quickly. The idea of spending too much time with this man was not a pleasing prospect.

"I want you to lay off the Mary Fagon story," he said, getting directly to the point just as she'd hoped.

"I'm sure you're aware" Charlie said "of the public's right to the facts and the free speech amendment, so I'll assume there's a more important reason for this meeting than the typical police-media head butting. Would you like to fill me in?" She couldn't believe how heavy-handed he had sounded. She hoped she had let him know how she felt about it.

He looked at her over his drink. The old phrase "if looks could kill" came to mind.

"A woman is missing," he said, "Possibly dead. The last thing we need is an amateur detective or writer or photographer messing around in the investigation. Didn't you realize last evening how dangerous that was?" he asked.

She hated his condescending tone. Despite her irritation she smiled. "Until last night I was not aware of the danger; that is true. On the other hand, this has escalated from a simple missing person story into something entirely more interesting. I have no problem cooperating with the police in any way I can. However, I will not give up what could possibly be the best story of my career." She kept her smile in place waiting for him to become angry.

He surprised her again by remaining quite calm. "I had the strangest feeling you were going to say that. And if you'll hear me out, I think we can come up with a solution. Are you willing to compromise?" He looked at her expectantly.

"Go on," Charlie responded. His willingness to offer a compromise was quite a shock.

"Okay then," Detective O'Brien began, "Here's the deal. Any, and I am serious about this, any information you gain you share with me. If you are following a lead, you let me know what that is. And nothing goes in print until I okay it first.

"Printing something in your article that isn't Okayed could hurt the official investigation. In addition, you hold off on it until we know what has become of Mary Fagon. If you do these things, you'll get an exclusive. That shouldn't be a problem considering the rest of the press hasn't caught wind of anything yet. We want to keep it that way."

Charlie searched his face trying to figure the part he wasn't saying. This deal seemed a little too good to be true. "Well, you've covered what will happen if I cooperate. Now let's cover what will happen if I don't." She knew something big was coming. He was giving a lot and seemed quite sure she would cooperate. She was curious. What came next made her breath catch in her throat.

"If you don't, it's simple. You become a suspect in last night's murder. I slap a court order on your ass and you won't come within one hundred yards of anyone involved. Clear enough?" He looked so satisfied with himself that, had she not realized how serious this was, she would have dumped his drink in his lap. In light of this, she chose instead to count to ten before responding. "Christ all... wow, you're good at this. You're right. My fingerprints, that unbelievable story. Shit, I wouldn't have believed it. Jesus!" she breathed. "Well, I guess you've got me by the proverbial balls. I must say I've gained a little respect for you." What she was really thinking was *'Oh my god! This is huge. If this man is willing to coerce and threaten her, she knew she was onto something big. Mo, she had it right the first time:* **huge!**'

He looked as if he might have laughed, but he didn't. "Thank you" was his only reply.

"You're welcome. Well, I suppose I should fill you in on my progress?" She had no problem cooperating. It sounded like the perfect situation. Plus now she would have an in with the local police department.

"First, how about I buy you a drink? Then we'll talk. You look like you could use it." He held up a hand and motioned for the waitress.

"Sounds like a grand plan to me." She turned and said to the waitress, "I'll have a Scotch neat." The waitress nodded and walked away.

# CHAPTER 14

It had been three days since she had heard a word. The sources weren't working out as well as she had hoped. The only hope she had for moving forward was an interview she had set up with Tarrin. The stripper friend of Mary Fagon had alluded to the fact that she may know more than she was saying. She may have vital information and Charlie wanted to get her hands on it.

Charlie resigned herself to waiting. Grabbing a novel off the bookshelf, she sat down on her sofa, tried to take her mind off the story she was working on and plunged into fantasyland. This excursion out of the land of the living was about a man trying to find out why six weeks of his life were missing. Usually this was a good read, taking Charlie away for hours at a time. Tonight this was not the case. As hard as she tried, her mind kept coming back to the strangeness of this mess she had gotten herself into.

"Maybe something hot to drink will help." Lately talking to herself had become a common occurrence. She went to the kitchen to start a pot of coffee. Coffee was her greatest downfall. She was sure someday that they (whoever "they" were) would decide it was lethal, therefore illegal and take it off the market. If or when this ever happened, she swore she would no longer uphold the law.

It was during this musing that the telephone rang. Charlie picked it up, "Hello?"

"Hi," a muffled voice replied, "I think you should stay out of it."

Knowing what it was about but playing dumb, Charlie replied, "Excuse me? I don't understand. Stay out of what?"

"I'm sure you know, but let me tell you anyway that if you don't stay away from the people involved you're going to cause more killing."

"What do you mean more killing?  Who's dead?" she asked, as her pulse rate accelerated.

"Have you heard from your little stripper friend lately?" he sounded almost proud of himself.  Charlie felt sick.

"I don't know any strippers." she lied  "Whom are you referring to?"

"Fine, play it however you want.  I'm just warning you."

"Why?" Charlie was afraid, but her curiosity was overpowering the need to disconnect from this malevolent voice.

"Because, I would like to see the killing stop."

"Are you doing the killing?" she asked, really wanting the answer to be no.

"That isn't a question that's going to get you anywhere."

"What questions should I be asking?" she pushed.

"The point of this phone call is to get you to **stop** asking questions." He sounded as if he was getting angry.

"Are you involved? Or just a Good Samaritan?"

"No more questions!"  No question now, clearly angry.

"I could be tracing this call...." she said angling for control

He cut her off. "You're not.  That is...unless your coffee pot is some New Age phone tapping device."

Startled, Charlie looked up at her kitchen window into the dark night. "Shit!"

"Don't get in too deep, Charlene, you may not be able to find your way out." The line went dead.

Hanging up the telephone, knowing she was being watched, she dialed the first number that came to her. Then, using the paging option, she dialed her number followed by 911 and hung up to wait.

When the telephone rang 15 minutes later she was ready to come unglued. She stared at the telephone, took a deep breath, and picked up the receiver. "Hello?"

"Hi, what's going on? You never call me this late. Hey, does this mean you want me to tie you up?" He sounded like he'd been drinking.

She spoke fast, tripping over her words, "Devon, get over here now. I think I'm in danger. Someone just called from outside my apartment. He knew I was making coffee. Please come." God, she hated the way she sounded. It was like begging.

He suddenly sounded sober. "I'm on my way!" For the second time that night the line went dead. This time it wasn't so bad.

The knock came approximately 25 minutes after the call.

# CHAPTER 15

When Charlie opened the door to Devon, she threw herself in his arms. He realized quickly she had momentarily lost herself in her fear. It must have been a horribly long wait, knowing someone intent on harming her could very well be outside her apartment just waiting for the perfect moment.

"Whoa!" Devon said, concerned. "It's O.K. I'm here now. I won't let anyone hurt you. Do you want to tell me what happened?" She stepped back. He could see she was appalled at her behavior. "Oh yeah, come in." she said.

After shutting the door and checking the lock she led him to the living room, sat down and motioned for him to do the same.

"I suppose I should have called the police but after the last fiasco I figured I probably should keep a low profile."

"I agree," Devon said. "Tell me about this call."

"I answered the phone and a man's voice told me to stay out of it. I acted as if I didn't understand. Then he asked me if I'd seen my stripper friend. He said if I didn't stop asking questions there would be more killing." Her voice sounded calm but Devon could tell it was taking some effort.

"He threatened to kill the stripper?" he asked.

"Yes. In so many words." she said,

"Do you believe him." he asked.

"What?"

"Do you believe he's already done something to harm...what's her name?"

"Tarrin."

"Do you?"

"I think he may have. He sounded so angry."

"Did you recognize his voice?" Devon asked.

"No," she said, frustration evident in her voice. "Don't you think I would have mentioned it if I had?"

"Maybe not. Think about it for a second. What did he sound like? Was there any detectable accent? You may remember something if you try."

Devon watched as she leaned her head back on the sofa cushions. She closed her eyes. He wondered what was going on inside her mind. Had she heard something in the voice that would help?

Looking at her this stressed was making him feel helpless. There had to be something he could do to help ease her mind. She began to speak softly. He leaned in and listened quietly.

"The voice was muffled like someone had put something over the mouthpiece. It was definitely a man. Deep voice. Strong, angry. I remember thinking that a crank call wouldn't sound so angry. That's it."

She looked at him, her eyes filled with pain. Devon knew she would hate for him to see her this way. He pretended not to notice.

"Okay, that's good. Did he say anything else?"

"Yes he said he knew I wasn't taping the call because I was making coffee. Or that... god! I don't remember the exact words, but essentially he was saying he could see me, that he was looking in at me."

"What?" he exclaimed. "Why didn't you tell me as soon as I arrived?" He didn't wait for her to answer as he headed for the front door. "Stay here!" he barked.

Ω

She could tell Devon was angry. It seemed so silly. What was he mad about? She'd told him over the telephone someone had called from outside, hadn't she? *'Oh, God,'* she thought, *'Maybe I didn't.'* She was getting more confused by the moment.

There were so many things that didn't make sense. She walked into the kitchen to retrieve the coffee she had left on the counter earlier, and sitting down at the table, began to sip. It wasn't hot but it would do. She was sure Devon wouldn't find anything. It had been almost an hour since the call. Not even a stupid criminal would wait around that long without doing something.

Devon came back inside, slamming the front door.

"I'm in the kitchen!" she called. While he had been outside playing 'commando' she had relaxed some. She felt more in control now and feeling a bit more than a little foolish at how apart she had come from a telephone call. When he walked in to the kitchen Charlie was stunned at how angry he appeared. She jumped up, almost overturning her coffee cup.

"What?" she asked worriedly. "Was someone there?"

"No. Whoever it was is long gone by now. I checked the perimeter of your building to be safe. Did you know from the hill behind your apartment you can see perfectly inside this window?" He pointed to her window over the kitchen sink.

She couldn't understand his anger; it made no sense. She tried to stay calm, as she answered, "No, I wasn't aware of that. I have not had a lot of time to scout out my neighborhood since moving here. I've been a little busy," she said sarcastically. "May I ask what seems to be the problem? You act as if I caused this to happen."

He laughed mockingly, "Didn't you? Since I put you on this story you've been in one mess after another and now it looks like you're inviting someone to do you harm!"

"What?" Charlie cut him off. "How can you say that? I have done nothing to invite some psycho to call and threaten me! Are you nuts?" she asked him, beginning to think it might all be true.

He looked at her and she wondered what he was thinking. One of his eyes was partially covered by hair that had fallen forward. Otherwise he seemed as well put-together as always. His hand raked through his hair, correcting the problem and his eyes met hers.

The intensity of his gaze was staggering and she could feel herself being drawn in. She didn't know how it happened but he was suddenly in front of her, the bright blue of his eyes reflecting her image. His hand came up quick and wound itself in the hair at the nape of her neck.

He slowly pulled, tilting her head back giving him access to her neck. He brought his mouth to her ear and growled, "Start protecting yourself, Morgan. I'm not always around to do it for you."

He brushed his lips against the tender spot just below her ear. Just as quickly as it had begun the assault to her senses ended. As he was leaving she heard him say, "Get it together, Morgan!" just before the door shut, leaving her breathless.

Later that evening, soaking in a hot bath, Charlie tried to figure out what had happened earlier. She had always known she was attracted to Nick Devon; although she had never realized until now to what extent. Now she knew he was also very attracted to her. She had had suspicions before, but he had never before made it so plain. Tonight he had crossed a line they had both drawn in the sand. She was sure that was why he had been so angry.

Had his protective nature made him aware of his attraction? Had that been why he seemed to project his anger at her? Her guess was the answers to all her questions were yes. She moaned and slipped under the water. This was not what she needed. She'd have to be very careful in the future not to rely on him so much. He was her boss and business and pleasure never mixed well. As her face rose from the water she decided that she was staying far away from things that didn't mix. The steaming bath began to work its magic and she felt herself begin to relax.

# CHAPTER 16

C harlie had a preternatural sensation that this was going to be a productive day. She needed to follow up on about a thousand leads. Dealing with Devon was also going to add to the mess. He was driving her crazy making things more complicated with his mood swings.

"If I could get my hands on that man," she said, thinking of all the hideous tortures one person could inflict upon another. The thought made her smile. A knock on her already open door broke her angered train of thought. Startled, she jumped.

"Oh, it's you," she proclaimed.

Devon looked pleased with himself. "And just how would you like to get your hands on me?" he asked in a voice that presumed far more than he had any right.

"If only you knew," was all she could say, for her mind was wandering from actual physical torture to erotic intimacy and back.

"Why are you here?" she asked, wondering where these conflicting emotions were coming from. Could it be the fact that he kept coming to her aid? It was probably the incident from the other night meddling with her thoughts. Before he could reply she began speaking again trying to calm her conflicting emotions by taunting.

"When I first met you, you were so confident, proud, ambitious, young and yearning for the best. Now here you are at the top, the confidence turned cocky."

"Cocky? Is that meant as a compliment?" He smiled. "Because if you were trying to insult me you're failing miserably." Charlie noticed that he had begun to walk towards her. He stopped in front off her and placed his right hand on the wall behind her head trying to pin her in. "I'm still waiting to hear what you want to do when you get your hands on me."

After her resolution not to mix business with pleasure, this situation was beginning to present a problem.

Charlie answered with the biggest smile she could muster, "Wring your neck, of course."

She couldn't take her eyes off his lips. They had the most beautiful shape, strong but the bottom lip almost pouty, just enough to make them very tempting. She watched them form words and realized she had not heard them. "Excuse me?"

"I said go ahead." He placed her hands on his neck. "I'd love to make your fantasies come true."

Charlie knew he was doing his very best to make her as uncomfortable as he could, so the only thing to do was to turn the tables.

Charlie reached up put both hands in Devon's hair and pulled his head down so that their lips were almost touching. As she spoke her breath brushed his lips and Charlie felt his involuntary shiver, "I'm not afraid of you." Feeling his reaction gave her the last bit of courage she needed. Leaning in slightly, she ran her tongue from one corner of his mouth to another. Leaning back she watched as his moist lips fell open in stunned silence. Before he could come to his senses, she ducked under his arm and left, trying almost unsuccessfully to stifle laughter.

# CHAPTER 17

All she could think about was Tarrin. *Is she O.K.? Has something terrible happened?* Charlie picked up the telephone and dialed Dream World. As she listened to the telephone ring on the other end she silently prayed. She prayed the prayer of the guilty, knowing or convincing herself that if Tarrin was dead it was her fault. Her pulse raced faster with each unanswered ring. The ringing stopped and she heard the familiar chime of the answering machine before the message begins:

"Hello, you have reached Dream World. All of our fabulous ladies..."

Before the message could end Charlie sat the telephone down in its cradle and wondered what to do next. She took out her notes again. Something was missing. This had gone from a simple missing person story to a murder investigation and she was smack in the middle of it. She needed to get Anthony Fagon's files. That's the purpose of the meeting she'd set up with Vail. Did that have something to do with his murder? *'No, it couldn't be'*, Charlie thought. The murderer had been surprised by her presence so he couldn't have known she was coming. Charlie paced the floor carrying with her the list of facts she had compiled.

"Think!" she said aloud. "There must be something!" What had the man said? She tried to remember the exact phrase. Thinking back brought up unnecessary emotions. She had been so frightened. Accepted wisdom would indicate that her memory should be faulty. Psychology 101, and yet the dark intimidating voice sounded in her head, the words were clear.

"The young lady you were dating without her husband's knowledge...." That was it. Damn! She should have thought of it before.

Tarrin had said "... someone Tony knew." Could it have been Vail? Was he the father of Kenny? If so what had the Devil been talking about, "using personal shared information?" Charlie grabbed her purse and keys and moved quickly toward her car. Meanwhile her mind tried to wrap around her suspicions.

# CHAPTER 18

The man sat alone in the darkest corner of the room. The moving spotlights over the bar occasionally passed over his solitary existence, quickly illuminating the shadows for a moment before moving to dust away the darkness. His trench coat was black and blended well with his surroundings. He wore a hat pulled over his eyes. To anyone who passed he appeared to be lounging, relaxed, shaking off some misery from a day's work.

In truth, he was wired as tight as a spring. He was waiting. This man was here for a very vital reason. He had a meeting that was to start now and his contact was late. This made the man very unhappy. He reached out, grabbed his drink and drank it down in one swift gulp. He sat the empty glass on his table and stood up.

Frustration mixed with a small measure of anxiety as he became aware of the conspicuous nature of the situation. Sitting alone in a bar, wearing a trench coat, it was so cliché. The entrance door opened, he paused.

A small man, the light glinting off his bald head, stepped into the bar, walked forward and pushed up a pair of wire-framed glasses to a better position on his broad nose. "Hello, hello! I'm so sorry I'm late. So many clients so little time. Chris, I presume?" He held out his hand. The larger man nodded and shook it.

"Well, Chris, I'm Alexander McNeally. So nice to meet you." He took out a small white handkerchief and dabbed his forehead.

Chris spoke for the first time, startling McNeally with the deep timbre and strong English inflection. "Let's get down to business, shall we?" he drawled. Few people discussed things with Chris as normal individuals did. Generally, his conversations were one-sided. It usually came down to begging. This was a pleasure he relished.

Chris had been accused of being mono-syllabic, yet when he did take the time to articulate using more words people had no problem paying attention. His enunciation along with the deep cadence culminated in an exceptionally startling experience.

McNeally stared up at him and smiled trying not to show his nervousness. It was obvious, he had heard stories of this man, but meeting him made him a believer. The darkness in him was palpable and frightening.

"Okay, then." McNeally said, and sat at the table "Your target goal has gone awry, and needless to say, my employer is not happy. Seeing that my employer is also yours, this presents a problem." He dabbed his forehead again.

Chris's explanation came quickly. "Vail couldn't be helped. Someone showed up. He went for me. I had to take him out." He stood looking at the nervous man and considered walking out. He was wondering whether he should turn and leave, or sit and finish the deal when the other man spoke making the decision for him.

McNeally nodded. "Well, that may be. Still, we have a problem." He bent forward and lifted a small briefcase, laying it on the table. He opened it and pulled out a legal pad. "Charlene Morgan." He said this looking up at Chris as if he expected some reaction. He was disappointed. Chris's face remained impassive.

He looked down at his pad saying, "They want her taken out. Apparently she's causing a stir. Sticking her nose where it doesn't belong. I assume you've done your homework and realized that she's the one that witnessed your little debacle? She's a reporter. The people we work for are not willing to negotiate."

Chris leaned forward, placing both hands on the table in front of him. His face was two inches from McNeally. When he spoke, there was no mistaking his feelings on the subject. "Let's get one thing straight. I don't take orders. I'm a free agent. I've come out of retirement for this job. I do it my way, or I walk." With only a whisper of material brushing the table, he sat in one smooth movement.

McNeally stammered, "Well... Well... then." He coughed and dabbed his lips with his handkerchief. He was obviously shaken; this pleased Chris. "Are you aware that someone else has been brought in, in case you fail?" said McNeally.

Chris replied, "Yes, our wires have gotten crossed. I can't do my job with someone else stepping on my toes."

"What do you mean? Are you referring to the dead girl?"

"Yes. I approached her, paid her off and she was all set and ready to leave town. Then she shows up dead."

McNeally was looking more uncomfortable by the second.

"I...Um...Yes, I can see how that would be a problem."

"I'm not in the habit of being second-guessed. My job was to find the missing girl and deliver her to her father. Vail was complimentary. I can't do the job properly if I'm not allowed to use my own judgment."

"I understand the family contacted you?"

"Yes."

"Are you aware that you come with a reputation for ruthless accuracy?"

Chris didn't reply.

"So you can understand their confusion when things don't go as planned?"

Still more silence. Alexander McNeally was growing more nervous and jumpy, as Chris remained silent.

"Okay. Therefore, this is the message. Someone is here looking for the same outcome you are. You may find they're a help, maybe not. I don't know who it is. He's someone who has been with the family for years. Your main objective is to find the girl. Let nothing get in your way. Your payment will be handled the same as always. Until then…" He held out an envelope.

Chris looked at his outstretched hand for a moment before taking the envelope. What he really wanted was to snap the man's fingers; instead he stood and turned, tucking the payment into the pocket of his trench coat. "If," he said, looking over his shoulder at McNeally, "things go wrong because of some amateur hired gun, I still expect full payment." Then he was gone.

Ω

Alexander McNeally had never been so glad for anything to be over. He stood and waved down a petite blond waitress. She sauntered over. "Yeah, honey?" she said sweetly, sugar dripping off every word. "What can I do for you?"

"Can you direct me toward the men's room, please?" he asked.

"Sure sweetie, just over there to your right, behind the bar." She smiled. McNeally walked to the bathroom, went into a stall, pulled out his legal pad and ripped out the pages he had been reading from earlier. He tore them into small pieces and dropped them into the toilet. Flushing it, he heaved a sigh of relief. He walked out into the bar again and looked around. He was still too shaky to drive. Sitting down on one of the barstools, he leaned over the bar and ordered a drink.

# CHAPTER 19

The first time Charlie had been here it had been raining, and the daylight had not yet come. This was an entirely different experience. Everything seemed less sinister now. She sat in her car, looking across the street where it had happened.

*'It!'*

What a crazy way to think of the scariest moment of your life. This was the place. The more she stared at it, the less real it became. Should she get out and cross the police barrier? Wasn't that the purpose of this little excursion?

"Okay. Get out; go inside, get the file, and leave. How hard is that?" She had hoped stating her intentions aloud would give her courage. It hadn't worked. She opened the door, dropped her keys in her purse, gripped the handle and slammed the car door. The sound made her jump.

"Oh great, now I'm scaring myself." The click, click, click of her heels against the pavement resounded in her ears. As she approached the front entrance she had a perfect view of the side alley. The trashcan was still on its side, as if some stray cat had knocked it over searching out its nightly meal. She remembered the pain she had felt slamming into its unforgiving bulk. Averting her eyes, Charlie continued toward the door trying to focus on the job ahead. Get that file. The yellow police barrier blocked the door. The front entrance sported a white sign, with the words:

CRIME SCENE

And below it a warning Charlie didn't take time to read.

She knew the risks and they were huge.

If detective O'Brien found out she were here, there would be hell to pay. Keeping that in mind, she quickly slipped through the front door. There were no lights to illuminate her journey. Reaching in her purse she pulled out her travel flashlight she had taken from her glove box. Turning it on, she continued forward. There were boxes and crates piled in every direction.

She hadn't realized that this was the warehouse that held all the Dealers Electrical Supplies merchandise. It was massive.

She continued forward, searching for anything that resembled the room she had been in previously. There were tiny rooms of to the left of her, each one containing a desk and office machines, but none seemed in order. This building hadn't been used as office space, yet some-one seemed to be preparing it for just that. The last door on the left was closed. She approached it, hoping this was her destination. Opening the door, she stepped into a small room with an open door on the opposite wall. Through that door was the room she had been searching for.

There were file cabinets lining the walls. Quickly Charlie began her search. There were files piled in each drawer, some to capacity. As she rifled through the files in each drawer, she stopped cold. There was a large mani-la envelope with the name "Carrie Pretton" printed on the front and below that in parentheses "Tarrin."

She pulled out the envelope and opened it. Staring up at her was an 8x10 glossy of the women she had inter-viewed at "Dream World." There were many others just like it, with bits of personal information typed on the back. Then, on a small slip of paper stuck to the last print, a hand written message: "Nothing here." What the hell does that mean? She looked through more cabinets. More of the same: pictures, file notes, all women.

She couldn't find a single file on any employee, or for that matter—oddly—no men were in the file. Then a thought struck her. Was Mary Fagon's file here? Had this man been stalking her? If that was true, was the affair story bunk? She searched frantically hoping to find something. Eyes scanning the names, she was starting to doubt herself when she saw the name. There it was, another large manila envelope, this one with, "Mary Fagon" typed across the front. She grabbed it along with Tarrin's. Then, scooping up as many files as she could carry, she headed out the side door leading to the alley.

When she stepped through the door, the brightness of the day temporarily blinded her, leaving Charlie unprepared for the shock of her body colliding with another obviously human form, this one much more solid than hers.

"Well, we meet again, Ms. Morgan. Didn't we have an agreement?"

Charlie couldn't believe her bad luck. She looked at him as her eyes adjusted slowly to the change in lighting. She was hoping all the while that the voice had been some guilt-induced, audible illusion. As he came into focus, she realized she was not so lucky.

"Oh...ah...Hello Detective O'Brien." she stammered. "How can I help you?"

"Well, let's see," he said, looking anything but pleased. "First, you can hand me what you're holding; then, you have the right to remain silent..."

# CHAPTER 20

The police station was dingy and overcrowded. The floors looked as if they had never been properly cleaned, as did the walls. Charlie sat on a wooden bench bolted to the floor. She knew she was in trouble. Looking around her she contemplated her fate. It didn't look great. She had been offered a telephone call. After much deliberation, she'd decided to call Garrett Quinlan. Unfortunately, he had not answered his telephone. Devon was definitely out. She moaned aloud thinking of his reaction.

"Anything wrong?" The question came from a young man sitting on the floor beside her. She looked down, taking in his appearance. He was sixteen or seventeen; he wore no shoes, only a T-shirt and jeans.

She answered lying, "No. I'm fine." Charlie was anything but fine. No family or friends anywhere in the city and here she was a criminal. Unfortunately she was about to be put in jail for being an excellent reporter.

Her parents would be so proud. She was grinning while she thought about what their true reactions might be. Her dad would slap her on the back and tell her she had gumption. Then he'd laugh and tell her he hoped she'd learned something from this. He always said that regardless of the situation, he believed there was always something to be learned.

"Charlie, girl," he'd say, "What d' ya learn?"

As long as there had been a lesson all was well with dad. But to not have an answer to his question, that was not tolerated.

She could remember many times when she was younger, before she'd learned the secret. Searching for that illusive lesson hidden in some crazy mistake she'd made, would drive her crazy. Now she was the expert. It's easy to find the lesson. The lesson she discovered was, never to make the same mistake twice. Simple. The problem was, she was a reporter, and so dad's theory wasn't working so well. She had been caught snooping. Isn't that what she was supposed to be doing?

How many stories would she finish if she learned her lesson today? She might as well give up, quit her job buy some cats and become a recluse. "Well dad, sorry, today I've learned nothing." she said, wryly.

"What?" a youthful voice asked.

Charlie looked down at the forlorn kid and realized she'd spoken aloud. He probably thought she was crazy.

"Just thinking out loud." she assured him.

He smiled and Charlie could see a gap where a front tooth had once been. "Know whatcha mean; I do that too."

He leaned his head against the wall and stared ahead as if they had never spoken. Charlie looked at the kid and felt a pang. *What had brought this boy kid here? Bad parents? No parents? Or maybe he was one of those that regardless of his upbringing had taken a path laid out by some trick of fate; some glitch in his DNA strand predisposed the choices he made. Whatever the reason, here he was leaning against this dirty wall.*

Thinking of someone else's problems was serving to get her mind off her own. Her heart had stopped its rapid pounding, and returned to its previous cadence. She had no reasonable excuse for her actions. This alone was causing her mind to jump from topic to topic. She tried not to ponder her future time in jail. Instead she stared down the long hallway in front of her and counted the cracks in the linoleum. There were many and this occupied her until she heard the voice she had been dreading.

"Ms. Morgan, come with me please."

Charlie looked up from her seat. Detective O'Brien turned and walked down the same hall she had been contemplating. She stood and followed. At the end of the hall, she began to wonder where he was leading her.

They passed what appeared to be several offices. Charlie noticed a desk in a large room, covered in files and large envelopes; they looked suspiciously like the files she had discovered that were taken from her. They continued navigating several hallways before stopping in front of a service elevator. O'Brien punched the button with the arrow pointing down.

"Where are we going?" Charlie asked trying to sound casual. She had visions of a huge jail cell, filled with the worst type of criminal.

"I don't remember one of your rights being, *you have the right to ask questions.*" he said, mockingly, obviously not willing to give any information.

She knew he was still angry with her. She clamped her jaws together to prevent one of her obnoxious quips to emerge and followed him into the elevator. They emerged a few seconds later and entered more winding hallways, ending in a small room with folding chairs and a chalkboard in one corner. There were photos taped to the wall.

As they approached, Charlie moaned and turned her back to the ghastly scene before her. "What is this, Detective?" she asked, trying to keep her stomach from backing up on her. The pictures were of women all in various stages of decomposition. She had only glanced at the myriad shots covering the wall, but had seen enough to make her ill.

O'Brien said, "We're working on a serial murder case and this is where we commiserate. So far, no leads. It's a disturbing case."

Charlie stared at him as if he'd lost his mind. Was this some sort of new technique for interrogation? She couldn't believe he would go to such extremes. "What the hell does this have to do with me?" Charlie said, appalled at his gall.

"Have a seat." He pulled a folding chair forward and motioned for her to sit. She blew out a breath of air, mumbling about crazy policeman as she sat, noticing he had placed the chair in a perfect position to fully view the atrocities she had seen earlier. She quickly averted her eyes. O'Brien dropped a file on the table in front of her as he sat down.

"Recently, there have been a rash of murders in lower downtown. All women, mid-thirties, all fitting basically the same description." He stopped speaking for a moment letting her digest the information.

She looked at him expectantly. He began speaking again slowly not wanting to confuse her. "Last night another body was found. This one didn't fit. She was younger than the others and the description was different. She had long red hair, very pretty. The other women were all dark-skinned, very ethnic. Otherwise everything is basically the same. Although I'm sure you don't want the details."

Charlie could feel her pulse racing. She started to feel nauseated as soon as he had started describing the newest victim.

Her palms were sweating as she stared at the file in front of her with trepidation. He reached into the file and pulled out a small baggie containing a slip of paper.

"When going through her personal items the detective on the scene found this."

He slid the baggie across the table. Charlie stared at it. She could see clearly a telephone number written across the small paper. Charlie felt sick. She was glad she had long ago digested whatever meager meal she had consumed, before rushing out to work this morning.

"Do you recognize the number?" he asked, already knowing what her answer would be. Given this piece of evidence, O'Brien had immediately called the number.

He recognized Ms. Charlene Morgan's voice long before the machine announced her name.

"Yes." Was all Charlie could manage as her eyes fell again to the file lying before her.

O'Brien continued, "In this folder, are pictures taken at the scene. I need you to look at them. Then I need to know how this woman came to have your phone number on her when she was killed."

Charlie had known this was coming. Still, hearing the words sent shock waves down her spine. She couldn't bring herself to reach forward. Her hands remained firmly gripped together in her lap.

Taking it upon himself O'Brien reached forward and pulled three 8x10 glossy photos from the folder and placed them in front of Charlie.

"Her name was Carrie Pretton. She was twenty-five years old. We think she was a stripper at a local gentleman's club. Do you recognize her?" he asked with no sentiment.

Charlie looked at the photos. Each photograph had been taken from a different angle. But all projected the same image. A lovely woman had been brutally murdered. Her clothing was torn and muddied; her hair looked wet and was matted to her head. On closer inspection, Charlie recognized it as blood. It blended in with the rest of her hair making it hard to tell how much there was. Most horrifying was her face. She appeared to have been beaten badly. One eye was swollen shut while the other peered up at Charlie with a vacant stare reserved solely for the dead.

"Tarrin." Charlie muttered, wishing desperately that she had taken the telephone call more seriously. She should have called the police... gotten protection for Tarrin. There must have been something. O'Brien spoke, snapping her back to the present.

"What was that?" O'Brien asked

"Her stage name. The name she gave me. It was Tarrin. I didn't know her real name... until earlier today.

Vail had a file on her. Didn't you look through the files you took from me?"

"No." he said. "This came up, so I put the other on the back burner."

"Oh." The hollow feeling in her gut was expanding.

"So this all ties in to that story you're writing?" he asked bitingly.

"Yes." Charlie decided it was time she came clean. Better late than never, she thought, hoping that she could somehow prevent any more deaths.

She began to tell him everything. First her interview with Mr. Fagon, the phone call that led her to Dream World, and finally the threatening call she had received.

He listened to her and obviously went through various stages of disbelief. By the time she had finished her story he was shaking his head and looking anything but pleased.

# CHAPTER 21

Devon stretched out his long legs and stifled a yawn. Long, arduous, draining, irritating day. He was ready to sleep, but not ready to dream. For the past several weeks he had been waking up from very disturbing dreams. It was only lately that they had begun to change somewhat. Now a major player in every dream was the one person he didn't need or want to be dreaming about, Charlie. She was driving him nuts, In more ways than one. He was not a fifteen-year-old boy, and he understood the ramifications of these types of dreams. As nice as they were, he was aware they spelled trouble with a capital C, as in his crazy, obsessive compulsive, workaholic, and stunningly attractive, new employee.

In college he had read a book on dreams. He remembered it instructing that the things you dream about are the things you need to work out in life. He didn't need to be into dream research to realize that his dreams were telling him he wanted her. That was apparent every time she was within thirty feet of him. Devon knew he was more attractive than most men, he'd used it to his advantage his entire life. This led to utter confidence when dealing with the opposite sex. But with Charlie, he never felt assurance when she looked at him. She always left him feeling just a little off kilter. Unlike the women in his past, he was never sure of her reactions to him. She was so good at hiding her emotions it wasn't until he touched her that his confidence returned. It was only then that her eyes would lose their focus and her pulse would leap.

He leaned his head back on the cushions and relaxed, willing his mind to concentrate on anything that wasn't Charlie. His eyes drifted shut. Her image came to life immediately. She was snarling at him as she often did. Then, inexplicably, he felt a pinching behind his eyes as his vision blurred slightly and he had the strangest feeling that she was in trouble.

Devon was not one to believe in the supernatural. He had been taught practical thinking in the Marines and later that was reinforced, by circumstance. Feelings only occasionally proved reliable. Tonight, reasoning didn't matter. His sixth sense was telling him Charlie had gone too far. This wasn't such a giant leap; she was always on the edge.

Something had happened. He picked up the telephone and dialed her number. No answer. Devon hated machines and left no message. If she were able she would have answered.

Good reporters always answered their telephones. If she was anything, she was good. He put the telephone down and tried to think of where she could be. Surely she wouldn't be at the office. He looked at his watch, 12:45 a.m. He dialed her office number. Again the machine; but this time he left a message.

"Damn it, Charlie. Where are you?" He hung up and decided the best thing to do was be proactive. He wasn't getting any sleep tonight anyway. He would camp out at her apartment until she arrived. One way or another he was determined to discover why she wasn't answering her telephone and where the hell this feeling was coming from.

# CHAPTER 22

harlie looked at the digital display on her car radio, 2:30 a.m. She had been at the police station all night. She felt weary and the guilt she felt over Tarrin's murder was enormous. O'Brien seemed to think there was nothing she could have done. He was angry with her for not coming forward earlier, but he was reassuring when it came to her part in Tarrin's death.

Very rarely does a person merit police protection based on one threatening telephone call. They had talked for what seemed like eons, going over every moment of her last few days. It had been exhausting. O'Brien promised to look for the Anthony Fagon file and allow her to read it. He had also demanded that she show him all her notes and extracted a promise from her that she would turn over all further contacts immediately.

She had promised this before and reneged. Although, O'Brien seemed to believe she was now more trustworthy, possibly because of her overwhelming eagerness to help catch whomever had killed Tarrin.

Charlie pulled into her townhouse parking lot and parked in the spot closest to her door. Her townhouse had a ground entrance and a small fenced in yard at the front. She opened her gate, never so glad to be home. Her body ached. There was very little to be said about police accommodations.

"Coming home a little late, aren't you?"

Reacting before her brain could assimilate the voice, Charlie braced herself on her left leg, bringing her right leg up and out to the side, snapping it forward with the force of a sledgehammer. Immersed in her adrenaline-induced attack, she hardly felt the solid block of sinewy muscle give as its owner collapsed.

"Ugh! Well, Morgan," Devon groaned. "It's good to know you can protect yourself."

Charlie's mouth fell open.

"Oh shit, Devon! You scared the hell out of me!"

"Well, from where I'm sitting it seems like I should be the one that's afraid." He pulled himself up from his fall from grace and dusted off his pants. Charlie giggled. She was feeling happy for the first time in many hours. Knocking Devon on his ass had been just what the doctor ordered.

"Glad to see you're so pleased with yourself." Devon said, genuinely glad to see her smile. She could see he was affected by her, it made little butterflies take wing in her stomach.

"Stunning." he said.

"Thanks, I thought it was well placed." she replied, intentionally mistaking his meaning. She was grateful when he allowed the misconception, no need to make things complicated.

"So, are you going to invite a wounded man in for some much needed R&R?" His white teeth shone in the moonlight, giving him an unearthly appeal.

"I don't know about any R&R, but you can have some coffee," she said sternly, trying to sound business-like again. '*Remember the rule*,' she chanted in her head. '*Business and pleasure don't mix. Business and pleasure don't...*'

She opened the door and motioned him forward. "Walking wounded first." She grinned mischievously.

"Very funny," he said, looking down at her intently as he passed. He made her very aware of how much bigger he was than she. Nick Devon was obviously trying to establish command of the situation. He walked into her living area and sat down on an overstuffed chair, putting his feet on an ottoman that didn't quite match. He watched as she walked by, she felt his eyes on her.

"How do you like your coffee?" she asked.

"Black."

"O.K. I'm going to go change. It should be ready by the time I'm done. Make yourself cozy." She left the room in a hurry her nerves making her feel silly. As she prepared the coffeepot for brewing she wondered what he was doing in her living room. The idea of him sizing her up from her décor made her uneasy. It was obvious she hadn't lived here long. No pictures adorned her walls and a few boxes still packed full, stacked against the walls. A fireplace looked empty and out of place. The mantel was unadorned by the typical family photos one expects to see. Putting work first while living out of a suitcase was her typical behavior. She was slightly embarrassed to have him see that side of her

# CHAPTER 23

Charlie took her stairs two at a time. She quickly changed into a pair of jeans and a sweatshirt. *'Nothing too revealing, casual, that's the ticket!'* Charlie thought. *'No sense in inviting danger.'* She stopped and stared into her full-length mirror. Her straight copper hair fell around her face, ending just below her shoulders, tapering to accent her large eyes.

Charlie leaned in closer. She looked tired, noting the red snaking through the whites of her eyes, making the irises appear paler than normal. She needed sleep badly. Her fingers slid from the corner of her eye to the top of her lips. She ran her finger over them, their tips gliding over the smooth surface. She imagined Devon...

She stepped back quickly, shocked by her thoughts. She could see the desire in her eyes, the slight flush of her cheeks. Her full lips fell open. If it were this obvious to her, wouldn't he see it? *'Oh, No!'* she thought, quickly turning from her image trying to deny the obvious. Her only hope was that Devon would confuse desire with exhaustion. She headed downstairs hoping that coffee would cure at list half of her ills, at the same time, hoping that the others would remain unfulfilled.

She wanted Devon; she accepted that, but he was the last thing she needed. When she entered the kitchen he was drinking from a coffee cup, propped up on the two rear legs of a dining chair, black boots balanced precariously atop her tiled dining table.

Charlie paused in the doorway. She opened her mouth to announce her presence but before she could speak Devon began to move. It happened so fast, later she would convince herself it had never happened at all.

Somehow his boots lifted off the table pushing the already balanced chair from two legs to one. On that leg, the chair spun 180 degrees and landed perfectly on all four.

Devon's feet hit the floor with a soft thud and a big grin on his face. As if having the balance of a circus performer was as natural as breathing, he stood.

Charlie shut her mouth and brushed past him.

"Coffee smells great." she said, grabbing a mug and pouring herself a cup.

"Are you sure coffee's a great idea? You look beat. Maybe sleep's a better idea." Devon said concerned.

"After the things I've seen, I'm not getting any sleep."

"The things you've seen?" brows rose in inquiry.

"O'Brien decided to arrest me tonight." Charlie muttered.

"What?" he said, shocked.

"Well, I guess I wasn't actually arrested. He just wanted me to think so. Fingerprints, phone call, the whole nine-yards."

"Who'd ya call?" he said quickly

"Huh?"

"Well, you didn't call me. Therefore, I have to wonder, who did you call?" His arms crossed over his chest defensively.

Charlie smiled, sheepishly. "Garrett Quinlan."

Devon scowled. "Good to know where I stand."

Charlie decided to change the subject quickly. "Did you know there's an unsolved murder case involving young women?"

"We've heard whispers about it at the paper. I've got Garrett on it, why?"

"O'Brien played a little 'show-and-tell' with me tonight."

"Show-and-tell?" he queried.

"Yeah. That's what had me out all night." She shivered, remembering. Unable to continue, she sat down stared into her coffee cup.

He waited, arms still crossed he leaned against the counter.

Charlie looked up and tried to smile. "Maybe I'm more tired than I thought." She continued; "Today I went to the office where Vail was murdered."

"You what?" He looked stricken.

"I went back to get the file."

"What file?"

"The file on Fagon. Are you going to let me finish or are you going to keep interrupting?"

"Fine. Do tell." He was getting more frustrated and she could see she needed to get through this quickly.

"When I went there, O'Brien caught me. He took all the files, including Fagon's. I thought he was arresting me. It turns out he took me to the police station and showed me pictures of dead women that have been murdered around town. Only, one doesn't fit his profile."

She stopped and looked at Devon. He was waiting for her to finish, giving her time to get it all out. She was holding things back; the files on Mary and the other women, the fact that Vail had been blackmailing them, or so she assumed. Some instinct told her to not reveal everything. She took a long drink, hoping he didn't notice her hand shake. She pulled the cup from her lips "This girl, the one that doesn't fit?" Charlie continued, "She was the girl I interviewed about Mary. I'd met her a few days before she got killed."

"You're not thinking that it's your fault this woman was killed, are you?"

"No. She sought me out. I'm sure it had consequences. She knew it was dangerous. I feel horrible, but…"

He stopped her "But what?"

"I can't figure it out. Why would someone murder her? It doesn't make sense. She already talked to me. What threat would some stripper pose? I don't get it."

Devon picked up Charlie's cup refilled it and sat down in a chair he had earlier abandoned. "Are you any closer to finding out why Mary Fagon disappeared?" he asked.

"I have some ideas but I'm not ready to talk about them yet."

"Are you sure? I'm a good listener. Sometimes hashing through the facts can help."

She gave him an exasperated look.

"Okay" he said, "Fine. I won't push. Just don't get in any more trouble. From the sound of things O'Brien isn't going to be so understanding next time."

"I'm sure you're right. Just give me a little rope. I promise I won't hang myself with it."

Devon shrugged. "Get some sleep. Don't worry about coming in tomorrow, work from home, sleep in. I'll call and check on your progress." Before leaving he said, "By the way, if you called Garrett, why didn't he bring you home?"

"He didn't answer his telephone." She shrugged dejected.

He raised an eyebrow and grinned. "Should have called me."

She watched him leave thinking, *'that's the worst thing I could have done.'*

Ω

After Devon left, Charlie couldn't sleep. Between the conflicting emotions and all that she had been through earlier today, sleep was nowhere in sight. She decided to write a preliminary story. For now, she didn't have all the answers. Hopefully, printing a simple missing person's story, addressing Mary's disappearance, might bring somebody forward with new information. She'd put a contact number in the article.

Charlie immersed herself in the story. It was basic and hard-hitting. Mary Fagon was missing, leaving a distraught husband and three children. She wrote about what a loving wife and mother she was. How no one believed she had simply walked away. She ended it by adding that an investigation was on going and any information would be appreciated. All calls should be directed to the office of Charlene Morgan.

When she was finished, she faxed the complete copy to Devon's office. That done, Charlie realized she was finally tired. Happy about this development she wearily climbed the stairs to her bedroom.

Ω

Charlie woke up suddenly from a nightmare. She sat up in her bed and listened to the silence. She was sweating. The house seemed too hot. She threw off her blankets. She needed water.

As she headed toward the bathroom she tried to make sense of her dream. It was all very vague. Devon was asking her questions. Rapid-fire gunshots were flying over her head. She could still smell the smoke. Wasn't it said that you had no ability to smell things in dreams? Whoever had said that was wrong. She had smelled smoke. She could still smell the acrid stench, stretching from that world into this.

In the dream Devon had been frightening. In all the time she had known him, there had been rage, sexual frustration, and irritation, but she had never felt fear. She filled a glass with water, and drank it down, enjoying the cold sensation slipping over her tongue and down her throat. *That's better*. The air not so stifling, she climbed back in bed. Staring at her ceiling, she wondered if sleep would come again. It did, this time undisturbed by dreams.

# CHAPTER 24

C harlie sat at her desk looking for any information she could dig up on Mary Lynn Fagon. She had been at her computer for hours, looking for information. She decided to focus on Mary. So far she had found very little. According to Anthony Fagon, they met in 1996 and married one year later in the summer of 1997. Before that she had been Mary Lynn Thomson.

No one Charlie had spoken to could give her any information about Mary's family. She was stumped. She pulled up the file from Social Security, inputting Mary's full name and her social security number. She waited. Her computer was slow, taking a few seconds for the screen to clear and another image to appear.

Mary Lynn Thomson had filed for her social security card in 1995. Prior to that, she had not had one. In 1998 she applied for a new card with her married name, Fagon.

Charlie stared at the screen. This woman hadn't existed before 1995. There were very few reasons a person would initially receive a social security number so late in life; most people received them as small children.

She wondered if Mary Fagon was not really her name. Maybe she had assumed a new identity. Charlie looked at her notes. In 1995, Mary had been 23 years old. From all accounts, she had been a capable young woman at that time. She obviously didn't come from the streets.

If that had been the case, she wouldn't have been able to enter mainstream society so effortlessly. Charlie believed the year 1995 was the key. For some reason, a young woman of 23 decided to become someone new in that year. Charlie felt sure she was on the right track. She pulled up the search engine "Google" and entered: "Head-lines, 1995." The screen blinked, the computer hummed. A list appeared. "219,000 objects found." Charlie moaned. This was going to take forever.

First, she eliminated anything to do with Colorado and its surrounding states. That brought the number to 192,720. She decided to focus on major crimes. Logically, a person starting a new life wanted to travel far. They would probably be running from something significant. This helped whittle the number significantly. They were now down to 64,240. She then discarded all crimes relating to kidnapping. She couldn't think of any reason that Mary would disappear based on a kidnapping. Although the numbers were looking better, now 57,102, still they were too high. She would never get through that many stories.

She separated them into categories: rape, murder, incest, abuse, drugs, hit-and-runs, pedophilia, necrophilia.

Charlie thought about the dates. Mary had filed for her social security number on August 19, 1995. She reasoned that Mary wanted to assume her identity quickly. That would mean she hadn't been here long before August.

That would also mean whatever had caused her to run, must have happened sometime in May, or June or July. She eliminated all crimes before May 1, 1995. The numbers came down to 38,068. She leaned back and took a deep breath.

This had turned out to be more difficult then she had imagined. She looked at her clock. More time had passed than she realized.

After her night of fitful sleeping, she didn't get to the office until noon. She had been lucky to make it in at all. It was now 4:23 and she felt no closer than before. She looked at her telephone. No calls had come in since she'd arrived. The little red light was blinking on her answering machine, announcing that she had messages waiting.

She had seen the blinking light earlier but had decided to wait before checking them. Her intentions had been to do a little research first. She hadn't meant to wait so long. Her eyes hurt from staring at the computer screen, she rubbed them, her eyelids felt as if they were coated with sand. She needed sleep, the kind of dreamless rapture you only receive after mind-blowing sex. That of course brought images of Nick Devon immediately to mind. She rubbed her eyes harder, trying to wipe away her thoughts.

Charlie pressed the button on her machine and listened as the monotone voice announced, "You have 3 messages."

The first one was O'Brien telling her that he would drop off the file on Fagon today. She would have until 7:00 p.m. to look it over. Then he expected it back on his desk. She looked around her desk. No file. Maybe he left it with Devon. She jumped up and rushed to his office, she knocked on his door.

"Come in." she heard Devon say. She opened the door and stepped inside.

"You look like hell. Didn't I tell you to stay home today?" he asked curiously.

"Thanks," she said sarcastically. "I'll try to look better in the future."

"That's not what I meant, and you know it." He waved his hand, dismissively.

"I had to work today. I'm already behind. This story is so convoluted. I'm trying to get to the bottom of it."

"I printed your story in this evening's edition. It was good. When did you write it?"

"Last night." she said sheepishly.

"After I left?" He was astonished. "When you were practically the walking dead?"

"Couldn't sleep." She lifted her shoulders in a half-hearted shrug.

"What time did you make it in?"

"Noon."

"Don't you think you've done enough for one twenty-four hour period? Go home, sleep!" he ordered.

With the mention of sleep, earlier images flashed in her mind. She could feel her cheeks reddening.

"Not yet," she said, shaking her head to clear her thoughts. "Did O'Brien come by today?"

Devon nodded.

"Yes, he did. He left this for you. Said you'd know what it is." He held out a large manila envelope. It was sealed with tape marked 'Evidence of the Denver Police Department.' Charlie stepped forward and took the file from Devon.

"Great. I only have two hours to look it over. Why didn't you tell me it was here?" she snapped.

Devon's chin dropped. "You were supposed to be home sleeping. I thought I was being kind allowing you to rest. I had no idea there was a deadline. O'Brien didn't mention it. He just said to make sure you got it."

"Well, there is a deadline. I have to have it on his desk at 7:00. That gives me less than two hours before I have to head over there."

"Seems like you're wasting time yelling at me, doesn't it?" he said, obviously not feeling any guilt. "Better get to it."

Saying nothing in return, Charlie stormed out carrying her newly acquired information. She felt like this file had been the cause of all her problems. This of course was unreasonable. But she didn't feel like being reasonable, she felt like kicking Devon in the ass!

Charlie slammed the door to her office, sat down at her desk, and opened the envelope. She pulled out the file marked 'Anthony Fagon.' The top page was his application for employment. He had been with the company since 1999.

There were six other documents. All were yearly progress reports. Anthony had been a good employee. No obvious problems. His production slipped occasionally but all of those times had coincided with large events in his life. They were all noted, the birth of his children.

Also in late '01 he had appendicitis, missing two weeks of work. Otherwise, all glowing reports. Nothing here. Charlie was frustrated. She threw the file. The papers scattered across her desk, fluttering to rest on the floor. She leaned her elbows on the desk, placing her head in her hands. She needed to go home. She had gone to the offices of Dealers Electrical Supply just yesterday. It felt like a week ago. Too many things were happening too quickly.

She needed to rest, and then maybe she could think straight. She stood to retrieve the papers she had thrown. One of them had landed face down and there was something written on the back in blue ink. Charlie bent, picked it up, and read the words.

"Wife's a looker. Great in sack. PAY DIRT!!!"

She stared at the inscription. She'd been correct in her assumptions. Elated by her find, Charlie finally had something to go on. Mary had been having an affair with Vail. What did "pay dirt" mean? Was he blackmailing her? Surely he didn't think Mary had money.

Her husband worked for him so he knew how much money Anthony made. Mary was a housewife. It made no sense. He had written "pay dirt" with three exclamation marks. For some reason Mr. Vail believed that his association with Mary was going to bring him wealth. Why? Charlie had no answer.

She gathered the papers, stuffed them in the envelope and left her office. As she shut her door, the only lights came from her computer screen and the little red blinking light on her answering machine.

# CHAPTER 25

Charlie headed down Interstate 25. Traffic was horrible. The right-hand lane was backed up from the Hampden exit causing merging drivers to slow the oncoming traffic in all other lanes. In her short time in Denver, Charlie realized the worst traffic was on this highway. There were only a handful of interstates here.

I-70 went east and west, I-25 north and south, I-225 circled around the eastern part of town connecting the other two. Of those three, I-25 was by far the most congested. It ran directly through downtown. It was the most central and everyone traveled this road, today it was more apparent than ever.

She glared at the time on her clocks display, 5:45; there was still time. The last thing she needed was to get on O'Brien's bad side, again. She would drop off the file, and then go straight home. She was finally making progress on the story. Maybe now she would get some desperately needed rest. Getting off at her exit she made it to the police headquarters with twenty minutes to spare.

O'Brien seemed pleased to see her. "Come in," he said smiling. She was amazed how a simple smile could change his face. He seemed almost jolly.

"Here's the file. Thanks." she said.

"Did it help? Find anything interesting?"

"Nope." she lied. "Just your basic employment information."

"Sorry. How's the other stuff panning out?"

"Other stuff?" she asked innocently.

He lost his smile. "I presume you have other leads. Care to share? Quid pro quo." he reminded her.

"As soon as I have anything solid you'll be the first to know." Charlie replied.

She felt bad lying to him. After all, she had given him the file in the first place. It was obvious to her he hadn't seen the notation.

"Glad to hear it." He didn't look like he believed her. He had good instincts.

"Have a seat. Want some coffee?" he offered.

"No. Coffee's the last thing I need. I'm going home from here."

"Sounds like a good idea. You look bushed."

"I am. How's your case going?" she inquired.

He raised his eyebrows. "Starting a new story?"

"Are you joking? I'm knee deep in my current project. Anyway, I would never get a story that big, that's Garrett Quinlan's arena. I was just wondering. All those poor women..." She let the sentence dangle.

"The case is leading nowhere. It's frustrating. I want to get the bastard that's killing them so bad I can taste it."

She could see he meant it. Charlie liked O'Brien. He had character. She believed he really felt for those women.

"You'll get him." she encouraged.

"Thanks for the confidence. Speaking of which, I hate to run you off but..." He motioned to the piles of paper covering his desk.

Charlie left, thanking him again on her way out.

# CHAPTER 26

It was eerie being in this place so soon after such a tragedy, especially knowing that the events surrounding her last visit, may well have caused Tarrin's death. Coming back to Dream World was a necessary evil. She had to find out all she could about Tarrin. She needed to know why it had happened. She entered and stepping through the front door a strong sense of déjà vu washed over her. She had been here before; everything was the same, yet it wasn't... Tarrin was gone. She felt that familiar sense of guilt. Three girls ranging in age from twenty-five to thirty were sitting on a couch facing the door. "Hello." Charlie said.

"Hi. Can we help you?" a petite blonde-haired person with big hair asked. Charlie recognized her from the night she had spoken to Tarrin.

"Yes" she said, "I think you can."

The blonde stood and started walking down the hall leading to a small office. Charlie followed her into the room.

"My name's Callie." She shut the door and motioned to a chair next to an old metal desk. Charlie sat.

"What can I do for you?" Callie asked, taking a seat behind the desk. The room was dirty. At some time in the distant past, the walls had been painted white. They had a yellow tinge from years of smoke saturating their surface. It was chipped and peeling in more places than not. Paper was piled on the desk, in no obvious order. An ashtray sat in the center, full to capacity; its smell permeating the room. Charlie wanted to get through this quick. Just being in this place made her want to take a shower.

"My name is Charlene Morgan." She reached into her bag pulled out a business card and handed it to Callie. Callie took the card and stared at it for a moment. Charlie watched for some reaction. Callie's eyes widened slightly. She looked at Charlie, obviously concerned.

"Is this about Tarrin? You're not going to put that she was a dancer in the paper, are you?"

"No. Not at all." Charlie soothed. "I'm actually covering the disappearance of Mary Fagon. Did you know her?"

"Wow. That's a hard one." Callie said exasperatedly. "We all go by stage names around here. I can check the files though. Hold on." She pushed back her chair, turned toward a small black filing cabinet, and opened the top drawer.

"What was her last name?"

"Fagon."

"O.K." She flipped through the files quickly. "Yeah, cool. Fagon, Mary." She pulled out the file and slapped it down on her desk.

"Oh yeah. Raven that's what she went by. Yeah, I knew her. Cool girl. Nice. Real quiet. She disappeared? What happened?" Callie asked

"That's what I'm trying to find out. She doesn't seem the type to just run away." Charlie was pleased by how open the other woman was being.

Callie's face lit up. "So you're like a investigative reporter, huh? That's so cool."

Charlie smiled indulgently. She pulled out her digital recorder. "Do you mind?" She nodded toward the device.

"Oh, no. Cool. Go ahead. But I don't know a whole lot. She worked a different shift than me."

"I'll just ask you a few questions. There's no need to speak in anything but a normal voice. O.K.?"

"Sure."

"How long did Mary work here?" Charlie asked.

"I'm not sure. Not long. Four or five months." Despite the warning she leaned closer to the device as she spoke.

"How long ago did she quit?"

"Oh, it had to be over six months, maybe more. She quit 'cause she was gettin kinda big."

"She was working here while she was pregnant?" Charlie asked, stunned.

"Yep. Girls do it all the time. She wasn't showing at all 'till like six months. I guess that's why she left."

"Was she close with any of the women here?" she asked,

A look of sadness crossed Callie's features. "Tarrin and her talked a lot. I don't know if they were really friends or not but, they hung while they worked."

"Do you know her husband, Anthony Fagon?"

"Tony? Oh, yeah. His mom and aunt own this place. He's a cool guy. They have another place like this across town. I think Raven worked there before she came here."

"Is that how she met Tony?" Charlie was surprised for the second time.

Callie shrugged. "Maybe. Like I said, I don't know her too good."

"What about Tarrin? Did you know her well?"

"Yeah. Tarrin and me were buds." Her eyes began to tear. she swiped the back of her hand across her eyes as she spoke. "We'd go out clubbing on the weekends. I can't believe she's gone. I almost quit when I heard she'd got killed. Boy there's some sickos out there."

Charlie nodded. "Yes there are. Do you think Tarrin's murder had something to do with her job?"

"Well," Callie paused, "Doing what we do, you just never know." She glanced at the clock on the wall.

"You said you almost quit work when you heard Tarrin had been killed?" Charlie prodded. "You sounded like you may suspect something."

Callie looked nervously at the door. "Well, there was this guy that came around. Maybe the day before she was killed. Anyway, I don't know what he said but she was plenty freaked when he left. Then the next day..." She stopped and stared.

"Can you describe this man?" Charlie asked slowly.

"Hell yeah! He was gorgeous, you know, in that bad boy sorta way."

Charlie grinned. "Yes, I know the look."

Callie laughed. "I'll bet. Anyway, he was real tall, dark hair, and he had these cool blue eyes. Can't tell you much more than that. I thought about those eyes for the rest of the night. Hey! Are you okay?"

Charlie could feel the blood drain from her face. It had to be some other gorgeous, dark-haired, blue-eyed man. "I'm fine. Thank you for your time." Charlie stood, grabbed her recorder, dropped it in her bag, and walked out of the small office.

Callie stood, startled by Charlie's quick retreat. "Was it something I said?" she asked the retreating form. No answer was forthcoming. She shook her head. "Weird." she said.

# Chapter 27

Charlie fumbled until she found the key she needed. She opened her door, climbed in the driver's seat, started the car, and pulled out of the parking lot like the devil himself were chasing her.

Why would Nick Devon come here? If it was him. Even as she was thinking it, she knew she was wrong. In her experience, men that look like Devon were not very common. She had spoken to Devon about Tarrin. He had no reaction. On the other hand, maybe she just hadn't been paying attention. Maybe he reacted and she just hadn't noticed. She had been wrapped up in her own problems. This was so strange. When she questioned Anthony Fagon, he mentioned another reporter.

What had he said? She tried to remember. She reached into her briefcase, lying open in the passenger seat. There were several CDs inside. She turned on the dome light and looked at the label. Empty.

"Great." she said, frustrated. There was a Burger King up ahead and she pulled into the parking lot. She pulled under a streetlight and left the car running.

She found the burned CD labeled "Fagon interview", popped it into the car's player and turned it on. After fast forwarding and rewinding several times, she found what she was looking for. She listened.

Anthony's voice was clear. "Sure, but I thought you guys had the list of numbers. I gave them to that reporter yesterday."

Charlie's voice responding, "What reporter?"

"He said he was from the Post. He stopped by yesterday morning just after we spoke."

Charlie again, "Do you remember his name?"

"Mackenzie. Mike I think. Yeah, that was it. Mike Mackenzie. He said he just needed the numbers, so I gave him a list."

Charlie turned off the recorder.

## CHAPTER 28

Charlie felt like her old self again. Confident, she walked along the street with a bounce in her step.

She hadn't had great sex, but she had slept well. Finally, she was beginning to separate herself from work. Charlene Morgan, consummate professional. That's how she had always viewed herself. Lately, she had let her perceived identity slip away, by becoming too personally involved.

She blamed Devon. She knew he intentionally put her on this story, wanting to see her flounder at the paper. She wanted to start out at the ground floor, proving herself, slowly climbing the ladder. She started a new job, in a new state, ready to prove herself.

Incredibly, she lost all balance the moment she laid eyes on Nick Devon. In an instant, she was knee deep in a story that could make or break her career. She didn't know whether to kiss him or kill him.

Last night, she went home and straight to bed. Her head had no sooner hit the pillow and she was asleep. She woke up this morning with new insight, along with much needed energy. So, she decided to treat herself this morning. She rounded the corner and entered "Camelot Coffee". She had been to this wonderful little coffee shop a few times, but never had time to enjoy the atmosphere. Always running in and out quickly, having just enough time in her schedule for a rapid caffeine fix.

'Camelot Coffee' was something straight out of a movie. Stepping through the doors was the equivalent of stepping through a time portal, straight into the dark ages, save for the constant sound of an espresso machine. The floors were constructed from wood planking. A long wooden bar sat against the far wall, bar stools scattered around it. Big overstuffed chairs were located throughout, beside small coffee tables, cluttered with books. Large, high-topped gray booths, lined the large windows facing the street. Small lamps dimly lighting the room, hung over each table. This alone would have been impressive.

There was more. The touch that pulled the whole thing together were the walls. They appeared to be stone, old gray and black stones, of all different sizes. If you observed closely, you could find small figures of fairies or gargoyles popping out of the cracks and crevices in the wall.

Charlie loved this place. She decided to bring her laptop to 'Camelot Coffee,' sit down in one of the large booths and relax; while of course getting some work done. She ordered a Caramel Machiatti with extra whipped cream. She selected a booth and plugged in her laptop. While waiting for her computer to boot up, she went the counter and inquired about Internet service.

"Excuse me." she addressed the young woman behind the counter. "Your sign says WI FI. I assume there are passwords?"

"Yes." the lady said. "It's $40.00 for unlimited or $10.00 an hour."

Charlie paid the $40.00. She didn't want to be rushed. She went back to her table, typed the passwords in her laptop, and began the search. She felt like she made progress before and started where she left off. There was a list of nine crime-related headlines. She decided to start with "Murder".

She pulled up the list of all major murder cases after May 1, 1995. The list was still significant. She clicked on the first one:

"Mother of two killed in drive-by shooting." She quickly read the article, No connection.

She moved on. "Man killed in homosexual hate crime." Again she perused the article, still no connection. She continued in this vein until her eyes were starting to feel grainy. Her coffee cup long ago emptied, hours had passed. The shop had filled and emptied several times. She got up and stretched her legs. She needed more coffee. After refilling her cup, she stood looking at the room around her. The whimsical atmosphere was exactly what she needed. Despite the current project, her mood was elevated. The goal was to resume her search, with the purpose putting a disturbing investigation to rest.

After another hour of the tedious process of elimination, Charlie saw something that caught her attention. The headline read:

"Death of a Twin."

Directly under the headline was a color photograph of two girls in their mid-teens. They were obviously identical twins. Charlie couldn't believe what she was seeing. Tallon Fagon could easily be one of the girls. The coloring, the facial features, they were all Tallon Fagon. Of course, Charlie knew that wasn't the case. Tallon was too young. The girls in the picture would be adults now. Beneath the picture was an article.

"*Veronica Jean Ashley (Daughter of Drucilla and William Ashley) was found murdered Wednesday in her family's home in Nantucket, Massachusetts. Mrs. Ashley discovered her daughter, late Wednesday, bludgeoned, lying on her bedroom floor. Her family (understandably upset) have made no official statement. Sources say the lead suspect is Veronica's twin sister, Victoria Lynn Ashley, who was seen fleeing the area sometime after the murder. Victoria is being sought for questioning. At this time she has not been located.*"

In the following weeks, more articles appeared. All of the articles alluded to Victoria Ashley having brutally murdered her identical twin. The fact that Victoria vanished after the murder only added fuel to the already blazing fire. The search was ongoing.

Charlie heard whispers about the Ashley family in the past. They were one of the wealthiest families in

America: also a very private family. Very little had been published about them prior to Veronica's murder. The Ashley's came from old money. Prior to her marriage to William, Drucilla Ashley was a Claymore. The Claymore's were more than a family; they were a dynasty. When Drucilla married, she took the prestige of the Claymore name and passed it on to the Ashleys.

Charlie remembered hearing that Drucilla had an identical twin, although Charlie never heard any details. She couldn't remember having ever heard the twin's name. What happened to her? Charlie looked at the photograph of the young Ashley sisters. History repeats itself, two sets of twins? She suspected one of those girls had to be Mary Fagon. *The one named Victoria Lynn Ashley; Mary Lynn Fagon?'*

Psychologically speaking, many people who hide out retain something of themselves. Was this the case with the middle name? Had she murdered her sister? If she had, how had she stayed hidden so long? With the resources available to the Ashley's, they should have found her long ago. *'Were they looking?'* Charlie couldn't imagine they had tried very hard.

She remembered her interview with Anthony Fagon. The loving mother he described. Could she be a murderer? She wondered how much Mary's husband knew about her past. He'd lied to Charlie about Mary working. He probably didn't want the fact that she had been a stripper, showing up in the newspaper. If Anthony knew more he wasn't talking. He may not have any interest in talking to her, but it occurred to Charlie that he might have spoken to someone else, someone close to him. Perhaps he had disclosed more details to a co-worker. *'That could work'*, she thought. She'd just have to find out who Anthony Fagon's friends were. She decided to start at Dealers Electrical Supply. She knew Anthony had taken an extended leave of absence, so there were no worries of running into him.

She wasn't sure which location he had worked in. She decided to take the straightforward approach. Charlie picked up her cell-phone from the table and dialed the Fagon residence. The telephone rang once, and then was picked up on the other end.

"Hello?" A man's voice answered.

"Mr. Fagon?" Charlie inquired.

"Yes?"

"This is Charlene Morgan, from the Post."

"Oh, yes, of course, hello. I read the article. Thank you. You made Mary sound wonderful. I know she'll appreciate it when she's back." There was a catch in his voice.

"Thank you, Mr. Fagon."

"Please call me Tony. I feel like you've done so much."

"Tony." Charlie said. "I'm calling to clear up a few things."

"I thought you were done? Didn't you finish the story?"

"Yes I did complete the missing person story. But I'm writing a follow-up story on the progress the police are making in locating her whereabouts."

"Oh. Are they talking to you? When he continued, he sounded genuinely shocked. "'Cause they won't tell me anything."

"I wouldn't let that concern you too much." she reassured him. "It's procedure. They can't really do a lot of talking. It could compromise their case."

"I understand." he said, sadly. "The waiting, it's just so hard."

Charlie felt bad deceiving him, but she needed answers and he wasn't going to give her the ones she needed. She plunged ahead

"I need a few details. You said that I could look at your file. Unfortunately, due to the death of your boss, Mr. Vail, I've had some problems locating it."

"Isn't that strange?" he asked. "Him getting killed like that? It seems like tragedies always happen in threes. I hope the third one isn't so close to home." She heard him exhale into the phone.

She agreed, "It is very strange. I'm so sorry for you. In any event, would it be possible for you to give me the address to Dealers Electrical Supply? The offices you worked at?"

"Sure." he said, "I don't think they would have it. All the files were kept at the district offices and they've all been shut down, temporarily, of course. You know, because of Mr. Vail?"

"I'm aware of that, but I was hoping due to the tragedy, files may have been moved to other offices. It's worth a try." As she continued to push, she wondered if he was hedging.

"Okay," he began. "I worked at 6000 Larimer. I was in shipping on the third floor. When you go, ask for Jonathan Collins. He was my supervisor after Mr. Vail was promoted. Johnny and I go way back. He'll help you."

After the past few minutes of dragging information from him, Charlie couldn't believe her luck. He'd given her exactly what she needed. "Thank you so much Tony. I'll let you know if anything turns up."

"I'd appreciate that." He didn't sound optimistic.

Charlie disconnected. Tony wasn't optimistic but her attitude had changed rapidly. She packed up her computer, left the coffee shop, and headed toward 6000 Larimer. The address was close and, as it was a beautiful day, and she decided to walk.

# CHAPTER 29

The large glass door ,was an intimidating entrance in an otherwise uninteresting structure. The glass was designed to reflect the world in a thousand different lenses, all woven together in an avant-garde design. As she approached, Charlie could see herself reflected *en masse*. A hundred or more Charlene Morgan representations, headed for battle.

The interior of the building was set up and decorated in the same creatively-enthused era. To her left was a set of elevators, all chrome and steel. She punched the 'up' arrow and waited, noticing lamps of different shapes and sizes scattered about; all were chrome with exposed amber bulbs. The doors slid open. Charlie stepped inside and punched the button marked '3'. The small space sported a large flat screen television, showing scenes from a wildlife preserve. Soothing music accompanied her short ride. When the elevator doors opened, there was a loud ping as she stepped out onto the third floor. The noise seemed louder than necessary, falling in line with her experience thus far. Odd how, one person's idea of décor was another's idea of ridiculous.

The receptionist desk was empty. Sitting atop the desk was a small bell. A sign beside it read, 'ring for service'. She complied and waited. A smartly dressed woman in her mid-thirties immediately came down the hall.

"Hello. How may I help you?" she asked sweetly.

"I'm here to see Mr. Collins." Charlie said.

"Have a seat. I'll let him know you're here. Your name?"

"Charlene Morgan." Charlie listened as the woman pushed a button on her telephone and announced Charlie's presence. A voice came back clear through the intercom. "Thank you, Allison. Send her in."

Allison smiled sweetly at Charlie and motioned to her right. "Third door on the left."

Charlie followed her directions and stopped in front of the appropriate door. A wooden plaque was at eye level. Written on it the name, 'Jonathan Collins' Charlie knocked.

"Come in," a clearly masculine voice instructed.

She opened the door and stepped inside. The room was decorated in grays and whites. Everything was in perfect order. The walls were bright, with a dark gray border accenting the gray in the light carpet. This was an entirely different setting than the ostentatious lobby and reception area. Furniture was sparse. One large dark gray desk and two lighter gray leather chairs completed the decor. Jonathan Collins sat in one of the chairs behind the desk, looking at her expectantly.

He was a young man, perhaps in his early thirties with short blond hair cropped high above his ears in a military style. His eyes were a dark brown, yet somehow soft.

He was a large man. She couldn't tell how tall he would be if he were to stand. Charlie guessed somewhere over 6'3. His obvious size would make him a valuable ally to have in a pinch. He smiled. His eyes lit up and Charlie decided instantly that she liked him. She walked over and sat down in the remaining chair.

"My name is Charlene Morgan. I'm here to ask a few questions about Mr. Fagon." She felt comfortable immediately, all ideas of battle and charging in gone.

"Nice to meet you, Ms. Morgan. Tony called and told me you were coming. I'm sorry to inform you, I am not in possession of Tony's file."

Charlie pretended to be saddened by the news. "Well, I suppose I should have called you first. I was in the neighborhood so I decided to just stop by. I hope I haven't wasted your time." She smiled, started to stand

and paused. "While I'm here, would you mind if I ask you a few questions?"

Jonathon raised his eyebrows. "I'm not sure I can be any help. What sort of questions did you have in mind?"

Charlie decided to appear unprepared. This interview needed to look as if it were not planned. She left her digital recorder in her purse. "Maybe you could tell me a little about Mr. Fagon's work record." She started with a question pertaining to the file she was supposedly looking for.

He nodded his head "Tony's a great employee. As far as I know, he's never had any problems here. I've only been his supervisor for a short time."

"But you've known him for a while?"

"Yes. Tony and I go back quite a way. We went to junior high school together."

"That's amazing." Charlie said honestly. "Did you start working here the same year?"

"Oh no. Tony started sometime after me. I helped him get his position here. He's done well for himself." He sounded proud.

"You sound like a good friend." She was hoping to open the door to more personal information.

"The best! I love Tony and his family. I'm heartbroken about Mary. Those poor kids." The corners of his mouth had turned down.

"I'm sure it is a difficult thing. Watching a friend go through such rough times." she prodded.

"It's so sad. They've been through rough patches. Then, just as they work everything out this happens. It's a crazy world." He looked sad and wistful for his friend. Sympathy for another's plight was etched on his face.

"Do you have any suspicions about Mary's disappearance? Maybe something related to her past?" Charlie watched as his face changed. His chin came up and his eyes widened.

"Do you know something about her past?" He spoke fast.

"Only what Anthony Fagon told me." she lied.

Jonathan looked disappointed. "That is really the only problem I've ever had with Mary. She never discloses any details about her past. It used to drive Tony crazy. She didn't even have pictures. No high school memorabilia nothing. How strange is that? A girl without a photo album."

He grinned, shook his head and continued. "After a while, Tony just quit asking. I told him to hire a private investigator. Find out if there was something she was hiding. He wouldn't even consider it. He loved her. He said when she was ready she'd talk about whatever it was. He said when you love someone you have to trust them. Anyway, it turned out okay."

For a fleeting moment, he looked angry. "Well, except for one thing they've always been happy."

"One thing?" Charlie queried.

"Just marriage stuff. We all go through it. They worked it out. Like they say, 'love conquers all', you know." He looked down at his hands. "I hope, for Tony's sake, that's true."

She stood and extended her hand. "Thank you for your time."

He pushed back his chair, stood and took her hand. Charlie looked up at him. She hadn't been correct in her estimation of his height. He was taller than she thought. He had to be somewhere near 6'7. Her mouth fell open.

He laughed. "I get that reaction a lot. Please just don't ask if I play basketball."

# CHAPTER 30

I t was a hot night. Spring was on its way out. A fleet-ing season, that didn't stop to ask permission before blending into summer, bringing with it the dry heat of Colorado from June to mid August. These were the times that sweat was welcome, cooling the body to some acceptable level.

Devon was on his deck, propped in a plush lounge chair, trying to achieve tranquility. The tension in his body ebbed as he sipped a cold beer, allowing the condensation to drip from the bottle onto his bare chest, mingling with his sweat, aided in reducing the heat. His body gleamed in the moonlight. A pair of comfortable, gray, cotton pants was all he wore. He thought about discarding those also, but didn't think the neighbors would appreciate the view.

Several times in the past two weeks, since Charlie had reappeared in his life, he had come close to altering their relationship. Taking it to a different stage. He knew he wouldn't have a hard time convincing her to follow his lead in the matter. He caught her looking at him more than once. It was always as if he were covered in fudge and she desperately wanted to lick it from his body.

When she looked at him that way, it was virtually impossible not to teach her things she had only dreamed of. *'But,'* he thought, *'that way lies madness.'* He took a deep breath trying to clear away all images of Charlie Morgan.

He took a long draw on his beer and looked at the night sky. There was nothing like darkness, blanket-ing all it touched, allowing only the city lights to illumi-nate, and making tiny stars appear on the horizon. The moon was full tonight, creating a warm glow, slicing through the blackness, turning the sky into a more pleasing midnight blue.

Earlier, Devon had wakened from another disturbing dream. He had been in the Marines, Located in some unknown wooded area fighting for his life against some unidentified enemy. As before, he'd woken up agitated and shaking uncontrollably.

The dreams were coming more often now. The images changed but the feelings were the same. Fear and guilt intermingled. It was never good. Tonight had been exceptionally tense.

Devon joined the Marines at age 26. Six months after graduating boot camp he was been pulled from his regular duties and placed in a special operations training program. The regimen had been grueling but what came after was worse. Now years later after shedding that life for a more subdued career, he hoped for a normal life. Normalcy, he craved it.

He had been tormented by memories replaying themselves in his dreams for a year after leaving his military existence. They finally subsided somewhat as things in his life reached a more consistent pace. Now they were back and Devon was miserable. He needed a distraction. Again, the image of Charlie Morgan popped into his mind. He was fighting his attraction for her and had been since the moment she walked into his office, two weeks ago. He didn't think he could hold out much longer.

Nick remembered how her tongue had felt as it grazed along the sensitive skin of his mouth. She was taunting him. He had been so shocked by her boldness that he hadn't had time to react before she was gone. Big problem, the alpha in him rebelled at any idea of being out of control. As much as he enjoyed the feel of her tongue on his lips, he hated the way it had played out. Control was and always would be an issue for him. He blamed it partially on his DNA and partially, the blame lay at the feet of the American government. *Damn training'!*

Why couldn't he be a normal guy, happy to let the woman take the lead? *'Because!'* He told himself *'I'm just not engineered that way.'*

The idea of taking control of Charlie physically brought blazing images racing across his mind's eye. An idea emerged. Maybe he should stop fighting his libido and go with it. It would certainly distract him. They were both adults. There was no reason it had to be anything more than two people expressing their animalistic urges.

He decided to put his plan into action. He would go to her, give her the option and see what she thought.

"Oh, that's brilliant." he said. "I'll just go over to her home in the middle of the night and say, 'Hey Morgan, how about some crazy naked sex'." He laughed, imagining the look on her face. *'No. Morgan needed to be seduced, thoroughly, erotically seduced.'*

He stretched his legs, swung them over the side of his lounger and thought of a plan of attack. When one came, he grinned. Pulling this one off would be fun. He only hoped the reaction would be a good one. If not the consequences could be disastrous.

Putting his plan into motion, he picked up the telephone.

# CHAPTER 31

harlie woke to the sound of the telephone ringing. She rolled over reached toward the nightstand and searched for the offending apparatus. Her hand found the handset. She lifted it and placed it to her ear. "Hello. Charlene Morgan speaking." She was still half-asleep, not realizing she had used her professional greeting.

"Morgan. It's Devon." a familiar voice stated. He sounded strange. Charlie rolled onto her back, telephone in hand and looked at the clock. "Are you aware of the time, Devon?" Her voice was thickened by sleep and slightly slurred.

"I'm coming over." It was a statement not a question.

"Why?" she murmured, still trying to assimilate the conversation in her fuzzy sleep-clouded brain.

"I'll tell you when I get there." Again she detected a strange quality to his voice.

"Is this about work? Can't it wait till tomorrow?" She was beginning to wake up now.

"No it's not about work."

"O.K." she said hesitantly. "I'll make coffee."

"No." he said. "Stay in bed. I'll let myself in."

She sat up, fully awake. "How the hell are you going to do that?"

"I have my ways. Stay in bed. I'll be there soon."

Charlie's heart was racing. What was he up to and why did he want her to stay in bed? "You're acting a little nuts, Devon. Waking me up, telling me to stay in bed so you can break into my house."

Devon's voice had taken on a deeper timber. "Morgan, I want to come over. Just answer this question. Do you want me to?"

Morgan was caught completely off guard. Her mind reeled. She was shocked. She couldn't believe the gall of this man, taking it for granted that she would lie here waiting for him. She opened her mouth to tell him to go to hell.

Instead she heard herself say "Yes." She heard the loud click through the telephone. He had hung up and now was on his way. *'What have I done?'*

She quickly jumped out of bed, pacing about in her room. She grabbed the telephone with shaking hands and dialed Devon's number with every intention of telling him not to come. No one picked up. She put the telephone down. *'Get hold of yourself.'* she thought. She'd just wait, then when he arrived she'd tell him to leave, or maybe she wouldn't answer the door. She thought about what he'd said. "I'll let myself in."

*'Great.'* She went around checking every window making sure they were locked; then moved on to the doors. They were all locked. She wasn't afraid that Devon would hurt her. She was, however, smart enough to realize what would happen if he came here tonight.

She combed her tousled hair and brushed her teeth, all the while convincing herself it was busy work. It certainly didn't matter whether her hair looked good, or if her breath smelled sweet. He wasn't even coming in. She kept telling herself this as she tidied up her room. An hour passed; she changed her clothes several times, finally deciding on a skimpy short set made from a comfortable flannel material. The blue-gray brought out her eyes.

She sat on her bed and listened for the doorbell. After another thirty minutes, she climbed back into bed and pulled her covers up under her chin.

Maybe he changed his mind. After all, it had probably been some crazy spur of the moment idea he quickly discarded.

She relaxed a little. She'd just close her eyes for a moment. She knew she'd hear the doorbell when and if, it rang. It took less than five minutes for her to drift off to sleep, a deep sleep.

Ω

Sleep was a safe haven. Memories and fantasies mingled and intertwined, creating a much-needed escape from everyday life. Devon was there, smiling at her, touching her, then gone. She moaned, moving slowly to find a more comfortable section of her bed. She couldn't quite manage to find what she was looking for.

She was tingling. Her mind was trying to grasp what was happening. Slowly approaching consciousness, the cloudy feelings associated with sleep were holding her under their veil. Something was different. Her eyes weren't opening. Sleep still held her firmly in its grip. She tried to turn onto her side. This proved impossible. As she tried again, the struggle brought her closer to the surface. As the sandman released his grip, her eyes flew opened.

# CHAPTER 32

Arms bound at the wrists, securely tied to her iron grated headboard, Charlie thought she was still caught in some erotic dream. Her feet were similarly bound at the ankles, effectively securing her to her bed in a spread eagle position. She moved her hips in an effort to discover her range of motion. When she heard a subtle moan, she realized she might not be sleeping.

"Finally awake?" came a voice from across the room. "I was beginning to think I was going to have to do the honors."

Charlie was remarkably calm considering her current circumstances. She was alert and awake now. Her eyes sought him in the darkened room. "Untie me," she demanded

He ignored her. "Although my way would have been more interesting. I love what you're wearing by the way. Sexy. Did you put that on for me?"

"No!" she lied. Charlie was beginning to get concerned. She pulled against her bonds causing her back to arch slightly. "Devon! I'm serious. Get your ass over here and untie me."

She hated the way she sounded. Her voice was low and husky to her ears.

Devon was sitting in a small chair, deep in the shadows, across the room. His voice again came from the darkness, "Relax, Morgan. I don't take anything that isn't offered freely." He stood walking toward her.

She watched as he came into the light. For the first time she noticed the large burning candle, sitting on her nightstand. It cast the room in a low flickering radiance.

He was dressed in black slacks and a robin's-egg blue, buttoned-down shirt, neatly tucked in at the waistband. A black belt with a simple silver buckle, met in the middle, showing off his flat stomach.

Charlie's heart beat faster. Her eyes grew wide as he approached.

He sat down on the bed beside her casually. His weight caused the mattress to dip slightly, allowing her hip to rest against him. Everything about his slow, deliberate manner screamed confidence.

"I told you I'd make your fantasies come true. Didn't you request being tied up?" he grinned mischievously.

She stared at him in shock. "Okay, very funny. You've had your fun. Now, let me go." she looked at him hopefully.

His hand came up and rested on her stomach. Her muscles clenched. He moved his hand up and under her small flannel top. His hand pressed against her flesh, slowly rising until his fingers grazed the underside of her small breasts. Her breath caught. His hand was radiating heat, vanquishing all reservations.

"Are you sure you want to stop so soon?" he asked, brazenly giving his fingers more access to her breasts. Before she could answer, he brought his mouth down on hers. His lips grazed, sliding, allowing her to feel only the texture of his skin. It was softer than she would ever have imagined. Then he stopped moving and their lips stayed pressed together, in what she realized was a challenge. Could she stay still? Could she send a message with a moment of non-response? She opened her mouth to answer the question and his tongue slid inside, mingling with hers. He was very skilled, the tip of his tongue teased and tasted, never delving too deep, teaching her, explaining the possibilities. She could smell firewood and taste muted butterscotch.

She pulled against her bonds. Her head lifted. His hand slid under her head bringing her closer. His fingers grazed her nipples, lightly applying pressure as his tongue moved, slowly exploring. It was so hot; masculine and sweet. She felt him shudder as she struggled to press her body to his. They both felt it happen. The moment she accepted the obvious, she belonged to him.

Somewhere underneath all of the tension she realized it was too much too soon, but she didn't care. He lifted his mouth from hers and looked into her eyes. A small smile of triumph touched his lips.

Her body felt raw, every nerve ending exposed. She had never been so out in the open. She had never been so turned on. She knew she should end this, she should be angry. But she wasn't and strangest of all, she felt safe. She understood that if she truly wanted him to, he would stop. Just the idea of this wonderful torture ending before it had really begun was unbearable.

She needed Devon to finish what he had started. She tried to find a way to show him. She couldn't tell him, couldn't admit that she needed him to finish this, to end her torment, yet she couldn't speak. She was ashamed of her need, yet being this much out of control was incredibly freeing. Without the ability to, bravely express those emotions, she decided to show him. Closing her eyes Charlie lifted her shoulders, and pressed her breast more firmly into his hand. She felt his hand disappear. The bed dipped and he was straddling her. She felt something cold, *sizzors?*, against her skin, then a ripping noise. The realization that Devon was cutting her clothes from her body made her reel with expectations. She squeezed her eyes shut tighter. When her clothes were removed, she felt more vulnerable than she could ever have imagined. It was like a roller coaster ride. She was climbing up faster than should be possible. She hoped desperately that he could keep her on the rails.

She felt his hand move smoothly up the inside of her thigh, touching, slowly rising to caress her, his large hands gliding, knowing instinctively where to touch. "Open your eyes." he ordered. She did as he said. Her eyes fluttered open. He was between her legs, one thigh draped over his shoulder. When had he untied her ankle? Before she could contemplate it further two fingers entered her deeply. She gasped, her muscles clenched. Her back arched.

"Ahhhh God..." She muttered, her ability to think slipping. Her eyes met his briefly before quickly looking away. Delicious shivers racked her body. His mouth was on her, drawing her tiny nub into his mouth, sucking gently. His fingers moved inside her. She was losing all grip on this reality. Her body writhed. She cried out things she would not remember later. Lights sparked behind her eyes as her body stiffened in a mind-blowing climax.

From somewhere far away, she felt his hands and mouth exploring every inch of her. Touching, caressing, tasting. It was exquisite. Then he was over her, gloriously nude. Broad shoulders, tapering in to a slim waist, a flat stomach, covered in muscle ridges. Long, lean, sculpted legs, she was mesmerized.

He untied her other leg and lifted them both, placing them around his waist. Their eyes met and caught. He entered her swiftly, his expression fierce. He was thick and long, filling her. She cried out, gripping him with her thighs. The pace was feverish. Both people lost in the intense race toward fabulous release.

Devon caught her mouth with his, possessing her, holding on as he moved inside her. Charlie moaned into his mouth, experiencing feelings new and unexpected. They moved together, sweat greasing their bodies. As he moved inside her, she felt his tension build, His body slammed into her with almost an animal fury. Her muscles welcomed the onslaught and she gripped his back with passionate acceptance. Time slowed as she looked up into his strained face and watched as he experienced the glory that wasn't his alone. Devon's body tensed, he groaned her name as he came inside her. She couldn't take her eyes off his beautiful face as he lost all hold on this moment and cascaded into the next. Unexpectedly she joined him again, leaving her body in a mind-altering state of being.

Devon collapsed atop her, quaking from his release. After a few moments he moved slightly, tucking his head in the crook of her neck. His tongue licked away a small drop of sweat there.

He whispered in her ear, "If I let you go, are you going to run away?"

She turned slightly so she could see him better then, slowly shook her head, still basking and smiled into his fabulously blue eyes. He sat up, untied her arms, and gathered her languid body against his.

# CHAPTER 33

harlie awoke to the smell of fresh coffee brewing. She moved into a long feline stretch. Her muscles ached. She felt better than she had in ages. Devon pushed her to the brink of madness the night before. They made love repeatedly throughout the early morning hours before dawn, resting occasionally, only to resume when their bodies had rested. She felt ravished. Devon was an incredible lover. She smiled, remembering things he had done to her. She pushed the covers aside and placed her feet on the floor; again she stretched, reaching high above her head. She decided to shower before breakfast.

Ω

Devon stood at the kitchen sink washing the dishes. He prepared breakfast and was cleaning up to distract himself from wayward thinking. It wasn't working at all. He had certainly obtained his goal. He was now thoroughly distracted. Unfortunately, he had discovered a flaw in his plan. He had hoped possessing Charlie's body would ease his overpowering lust for her, effectively getting her out of his system. It hadn't worked. It had profoundly backfired. He wanted her now, more than ever. Last night he couldn't get enough of her. Seeing her bound and so wonderfully naked almost sent him careening over the proverbial edge.

The sex had been the best he'd ever had. He wanted more. When he woke up with her in his arms, it was all he could do not to wake her up and repeat the events from the night before. He quickly decided against it. He still wasn't sure how she would react to him in the light of day. He knew he had seduced her, effectively taken her without any thought of the future. He hoped she wouldn't hold it against him.

Charlie entered the kitchen. Devon turned and looked at her grinning. "Hey there, sleepy head. Coffee?"

"Thanks." She took the mug and sipped the steaming liquid, her eyes taking him in over the edge of the mug.

"I've prepared breakfast. Hope you like omelets."

She sat at the table and he placed a delicious-looking concoction in front of her.

He watched her take a bite. She wore a small white T-shirt, no bra and a pair of very low cut, snug jeans. Her feet were bare; her hair was damp, falling loosely around her shoulders. She looked younger than her 29 years. He wanted to be a cave man, grab her by the hair, drag her up stairs and ravish her. He would keep her tied to his bed so no other man would ever see her this way and he could have her whenever he wanted.

"Aren't you going to join me?" She motioned to the plate across from her.

He nodded and sat, feeling stressed by his barbarian thoughts. Is this all she was going to bring out in him now? Was he going to become possessive, obsessive and sexually insatiable? He found that he was staring. They ate in silence, each waiting for the other to say something to ease the tension.

Charlie spoke first. "I've got a lot of work to do today. I should get to it." She was feeling uncomfortable and it showed.

He watched as she stood and placed her dirty dish in the sink. The scrape of his chair was too loud as he left the table.

He stood behind her. Her hands started to shake and the plate fell into the sink, splashing into the warm soapy water. His hands came around her, grasping her hands in his, stilling them. His body was pressed against her back. He inhaled the scent of her hair. She smelled like peaches and something else, a spice he couldn't place.

He whispered in her ear, "We can handle this, Morgan, there's nothing to it." He turned her around. He was assuring himself as much as her.

Ω

Charlie looked into his eyes and knew she was lost. Her heart swelled as she recognized the emotion she was feeling. It scared her to death.

This overwhelming, cocky, demanding man standing before her was the man she loved. Her breath caught in her throat. She knew it as if it were branded on her heart. She loved him! Even though her heart ached with the knowledge, *'I won't tell him.'* she thought, demanding her mind to command her mouth.

She'd always known Nicholas Devon didn't fall in love. He was the "love 'em and leave 'em" type. She could see it in his eyes. Passion, lust, but not love. She stood on the tips of her toes and kissed him. She'd take what she could get, for now. But he could never know. She couldn't bare the humiliation of the rejection that would most assuredly follow.

# CHAPTER 34

Andrew McNeally sat in an over-sized leather chair in the study of the Ashley's Victorian mansion. He watched as William Ashley paced, ranting about what little progress had been made.

Andrew was nervous. He was accustomed to this condition. He felt as if he had been nervous since the day he was born. His size and the fact that his hair had begun falling out before he had turned thirty only intensified his inferiority complex; in fact, it added greatly to his nervousness.

He dabbed his forehead with a handkerchief, a nervous habit that William Ashley detested.

"Will you please stop that?" Ashley scolded. "Have you been listening to me?"

"Yes, Sir." McNeally answered nervously, tucking the handkerchief into his jacket pocket.

"Good. What are you going to do to fix the problem?"

William Ashley was unaccustomed to problems. He had been living off others for as long as he could remember. For twenty years he'd gotten by on his looks.

Then he'd met the Claymore sisters and all his problems had been in the past. For more than 30 years he had been married to Drucilla Claymore and in all that time he had been problem free. Except of course for the horrible debacle involving his daughters.

He'd waited for over nine years to take care of this mess and now everything was falling apart. He slammed his fist on the large mahogany desk and turned, facing McNeally.

"Goddamn it, man! I sent you out there to make sure that this was taken care of! What's the damn problem?"

"Well... ah," he stammered. "There seems to be a reporter digging up background information. She's talking to everyone who knew Victoria. She's getting closer."

"What's the problem? Send your man to take care of her."

"We can't keep doing that. We have contacts in Denver. The situation is getting hot. Two people have already been killed."

Ashley's face turned red. His blue eyes squinted at McNeally.

"Have you lost your head? Things can't get much hotter. Have the bitch killed!"

Andrew McNeally could see that Ashley was coming apart at the seams. Normally, he appeared the perfect gentleman. Dressed impeccably, his six-foot-frame was impressive. Under normal circumstances this was a distinguished looking man.

Now his silver hair was tousled. He still wore the same suit he had worn yesterday.

Before McNeally could respond, the door to the study opened. Drucilla Ashley walked into the room, as a queen would enter her throne room. She moved with the grace and elegance reserved for those reared with all that money could provide.

Drucilla was a handsome woman of fifty-one years. Her long mane of blond hair was secured at the nape of her neck with a silver clasp. Her make-up was perfect, as was her clothing; from head to toe she was the personification of a wealthy aristocrat.

She waved her hand in the air. "Lord, William. What's all this racket? The servants are all agog." She glided over to her husband and touched his sleeve. "Darling, you must calm down." She smiled sweetly into his eyes.

Ashley's demeanor immediately changed. He bent down and placed a light kiss on her upturned cheek. "Of course. I was just speaking to Mr. McNeally here about our current predicament."

Drucilla turned and smiled at McNeally.

"Hello, Andrew. How are you today?"

"Fine, Mrs. Ashley." He nodded and dabbed his head.

"I hope William here isn't causing you too much stress." She turned to Ashley. "Are you, darling?"

"No. I think McNeally and I have come to an understanding." He looked at McNeally. "Haven't we?" There was an unspoken message in those words.

"Of course... of course. Completely. I understand." He stood, gathering his leather briefcase. "Is that all?" he asked, hoping it was.

Drucilla answered. "That will be all, Andrew. Thank you so much for stopping by. Please let us know when any progress has been made locating Victoria."

"As soon as I know anything." McNeally said, already heading for the door.

Ashley made a low sound in his throat obviously disgusted with McNeally.

"Why do we have to have that pitiful little man working for us?" he asked.

Drucilla looked at her husband as if he were a small child.

"I've already explained this to you, sweetheart. He's been with my family for years. We need someone who can be trusted. Andrew is that man. Where else is he going to earn the money we've been paying him?"

"But, Drucilla," he said, letting a whine slip into his voice.

Her eyes grew cold. "I've asked you repeatedly not to call me that when we're alone."

"Sorry, honey. Old habits." He lifted his shoulders and walked around his desk, practically falling into his chair. "I detest that man. In addition, what is that thing he's always doing? Cleaning his head?"

"Oh, William. Relax. I told you it's settled. Now go and change your suit. We have a luncheon appointment at two o' clock and I won't be seen with you looking like that."

"Lunch? With who?"

"We are lunching with the president of the yacht club and his wife."

"Cancel it. Or better yet, go without me." He leaned his head back and stared at the ceiling.

"I will do no such thing. How will it look if I show up alone? It's very important for things to appear normal, especially now." Her tone left no room for argument. "Go change your suit. I'll have Jim pull the car around in fifteen minutes." That said, she turned and left the room.

Ω

William Ashley sat at his desk, watching as his wife left the room. He had every intention of doing as she asked. He always did. Everyone knew that, in any given situation, he was the man with the power, except concerning Drucilla. She had power over him. He didn't mind. He knew that behind every great man was an even greater woman. He had come to believe in that statement a great deal.

Ashley knew that he would never have come so far without his wonderful wife. Still, even Drucilla couldn't control some things.

He picked up the telephone and dialed. A man's voice answered immediately. Ashley wasted no time in announcing himself.

"I want the reporter taken out. You have forty-eight hours. And find Victoria."

"Yes sir."

"No screw ups. I can't wait much longer."

"I understand."

"I hope you do. Things are not good. The reports I'm receiving are leaving quite a lot to be desired."

"Yes sir. When will payment be in place?"

"The moment you tell me you've located Victoria." Ashley snapped.

"That will be soon."

"It had better be. When I get that call, I'll take care of plane tickets and your financial arrangements."

"Understood, sir."

"Another thing."

"Yes sir?"

"Tie up all loose ends. McNeally has someone else on this."

"I'm aware of that sir."

"Good. That'll make it easier. Drucilla has something on this person. He's good. He also knows too much."

"What course of action do you want me to take, sir?"

"Make it look like he's gone over the edge. Too much pressure or something."

"Anything specific?"

"Damn it man. Isn't that what I pay you for?"

"Yes sir."

"Set the bastard up, then kill him."

"Anything else, sir?"

"No. Just do it soon or the deal's off."

Ashley was bluffing. He needed to feel like he was in control. Now nothing could be farther from the truth.

He hung up the telephone, looked at his watch, and stood. He had less than ten minutes.

# CHAPTER 35

The offices were dark. The lights had shut down hours ago. Charlie was the last employee in the building. She decided to work late on a whim, her notes scattered about the floor. She sat in the midst of her papers trying to sort out the mess. Two days had passed since her night with Devon. The first day she had immersed herself in work, doing anything to occupy herself. When she arrived home, she expected to hear from him. He hadn't called.

Now she was convinced he was avoiding her. Maybe he had seen it in her eyes, she thought, not for the first time. Maybe some emotion that had scared him off. She felt like a high school girl waiting to be asked to prom. This was what she had dreaded. How had she let this happen? All she had to do was say no. But she hadn't and now she was mooning over some gorgeous guy that had obviously used her. She put her head in her hands and groaned. "Oh no... I'm so stupid!"

She shook off her distracting thoughts. Tried to clear her mind and concentrated on the problem at hand. Charlie hoped focusing on what had become an intriguing mystery, would help. She was sure of several things

*Mary Fagon had vanished.

*Mary Fagon was Victoria Ashley, Wanted for questioning in the death of her twin sister.

*Anthony Fagon loved his wife but knew nothing of her past.

*Little Kenny was not Mr. Fagon's biological child.

*Mary was having an affair with Carl Vail, Anthony Fagon's boss.

*Carl Vail had been blackmailing Mary, along with other women.

*Tarrin, Carrie Pretton, was also being blackmailed.

*Tarrin was murdered.

* Lastly but importantly -Someone wanted Charlie off this story.

She knew these things. The things she didn't know were driving her crazy. Who killed Carl Vail and Carrie Pretton? Why had they been killed?

Did Carl Vail know Mary's identity? Is that why he had been blackmailing her? On the other hand, was it just the affair? If that were the case, had the blackmailing stopped before she'd disappeared? Once Anthony knew about Mary and Vail, there wouldn't have been anything left to hold over her head. Who was the man who had questioned Carrie Pretton before she was murdered? All of these questions and more swam through Charlie's mind. She was running out of people to talk to.

One possibility rose in Charlie's mind. If Mary suspected that someone knew about her past, she may have gone into hiding. She had run away once, maybe she had reverted to form. Something about that didn't seem quite right. Too many players were involved, there were definitely people behind the scenes, because, murders had been committed. Charlie remembered the ominous telephone call she received. Whoever placed that call, killed Carrie Pretton, she was sure of that.

She needed to speak to someone in the Ashley family. Maybe they had heard from Mary. If not, she didn't have to let on that she knew anything. She would tell them she was doing a follow-up story on the murder and any progress being made. That should cover her tracks. That decided, she packed up her notes, throwing them in her briefcase and prepared to go home for the night. She would make calls first thing in the morning concerning flights to Nantucket.

Carrying her briefcase she shut off her lights and quickly left her office. The building was silent. Her heels clacked against the tile as she walked down the long hall leading to the lobby. The sound echoed, filling the silence. Passing several open office doors, she glanced into Garrett Quinlan's; surprised he wasn't in. He never came in early and he always worked late. *'The price of success.'*

Charlie paused. She heard something behind her. A low, knocking sound. "Is anyone there?" she called out. *'No answer.'* Her pace quickened. She felt the hairs on the nape of her neck stand up. Someone was in the building. *'Friend or foe?'* She didn't know. She wasn't willing to stick around and find out.

She turned the corner, the hall opened into a large lobby. Art-deco style chairs and small tables littered the room, illuminated by small lights in the corners that stayed on after hours. She fished her keys out of her purse and unlocked the large glass door.

Something hit her hard in the center of her back, pushing her through the door and out into the night. She stumbled, but somehow regained her footing. Her briefcase flew from her hand and fell open on the sidewalk. Her notes were strewn across the pavement. She gasped and started to turn. A strong arm reached around her neck in a strangle hold. She tried to scream but her constricted throat only allowed a high-pitched shriek to emerge. Her right arm was wrenched behind her at an impossible angle causing her eyes to water. The pain shot through her immobilizing her as her body was pressed forward, slamming her solar plexus against a parked car. She whimpered, tears now flowing freely.

Her mind screamed. She'd taken martial arts and other self-defense classes but nothing prepared her for this. This was a blitz attack by a professional. She tried to drop her weight as she had been taught, but he held her without reacting. Whoever had her was strong, too strong for her to fight.

"I warned you to stay out of this," a gravely voice said in her ear. "Now it's too late."

Charlie suspected she was going to die. At that moment she decided to go down, fighting. A new surge of strength emerged, but before she could take any action, the body holding her was torn away violently. Charlie crumpled to the ground as air rushed into her lungs. She was on her hands and knees. As she turned and looked over her shoulder, what she saw shocked her to the core.

A husky man in a trench coat and ski mask was trying unsuccessfully to protect himself from the devastating punishment he was receiving. Nicholas Devon jumped into the air, spun, landing a bone crunching kick to the side of the other man's face. His head snapped to the side, his limp body falling hard to the pavement. Devon stood stoic as a mythic Greek statue, contemplating his opponent for several moments before turning toward Charlie.

She was leaning against the side of the parked car she had been slammed against earlier, a small weak smile playing across her tear-streaked face. Charlie had never been so happy to see anyone in her life.

"What the hell are you doing here alone at night?" he said angrily.

"You're angry at me?" she croaked, her voice gravelly, still recovering from the attack.

He bent down and lifted her in a crushing embrace. "Damn it, Morgan," she heard his voice crack. "If anything had happened to you..." he left his sentence unfinished.

Charlie pressed herself closer to him. She didn't understand his anger. She didn't understand much at all. However, she felt safe, again, which was all that mattered.

# CHAPTER 36

Devon was furious. Charlie's attacker had disappeared. He came close to killing the bastard. He had only stopped himself because Charlie had been there. Witnessing any man put his hands on her, and in violence, made Devon lose all sense of his present life. He had been prepared to kill the man, one breath from total annihilation. Then he remembered where he was: standing in front of the Denver Post offices, with Charlie not ten feet away, watching him, tears streaming down her beautiful face.

"Fuck!" he punched the swinging bag again, cursing as his knuckles split open, blood smearing on the canvas covering. He had been working out for over an hour. Sweat dripped into his eyes. His muscles bunched and strained as he moved. His leg whipped out knocking the bag, only to repeat the same move as it swung forward into range. His rage was bubbling to the surface.

His vision clouded. A scene flashed in his mind, Morgan being slammed against a car, her body going limp. He jumped into the air twisting his body, his leg whipping out, reenacting that last blow, watching in his mind's eye, as the attacker slumped to the ground.

In his vivid imagination the scene changed, unlike the previous battle, this one ended differently. His body slammed forward, punching blow by blow as he envisioned plunging a knife into the attacker's heart, twisting the knife, watching as the lifeblood left the other man's body. As he felt another rip open up on his knuckles, Devon snapped into the present. Slick with sweat, his breath coming in and out in great heaving movements. He bent grabbing a thigh with each hand trying to regulate his breathing. He stood slowly. The bag swung in long arching movements and blood speckled the canvas from his torn knuckles.

He reached out, grabbed the bag and stilled it. He leaned in that position a moment before turning and walking from the room. Devon entered his bathroom, shed his clothing and stepped into the shower. The steaming water felt good as it beat against his tortured muscles. However it did nothing for his tortured soul.

He stepped from the shower, dried off, and bandaged his torn knuckles. That done, he contemplated going to Charlie. He knew she would be angry. He left so abruptly the night before. He quickly discarded the idea, remembering how everything shut down when he was near her. Devon had been with women before, yet, nothing prepared him for Charlie Morgan. Now more than ever, he needed to stay focused. Her life was in danger. Maybe after she finished the story, he thought, maybe then he could tolerate the distraction, but not now. She needed him. That much was obvious. He just hoped that after the way he had treated her, she would still want him.

He fell onto his bed, throwing one arm over his eyes. He contemplated making her understand his coldness. He groaned. Since the day she walked into his office nothing had been simple.

He knew he couldn't be near her; still, soon he would stay close, if only to protect her. But, tonight, while he gained some perspective, the police would take care of that. He knew other ways to ensure her safety. His dilemma would be carrying them out.

# CHAPTER 37

The bruise was a vivid purple and ran the length of her throat angling down from ear to collar bone.

She stared at her image in the mirror. Touching the purple area gingerly, she remembered the horrible pressure as the man strangled her. Her voice still held obvious signs of her attack. The physician had assured her the rasping gravelly sound would diminish as her larynx healed. He also told her to expect it to look worse before it got better, a very common occurrence with severe bruising in this area; otherwise, physically no serious harm had been done. Her mental status was an entirely different story. Suspecting that someone was going to do you harm and knowing it, were two very different things.

The threatening telephone call had done its job, frightening Charlie, especially after she'd realized whomever was calling was doing so while watching her through the window. Then seeing pictures of Carrie Pretton beaten to death had shaken her up; that had rapidly taken her fear to a different level.

Now things had changed. The focus had shifted to her. No longer were people around her being threatened, it had now become violently personal.

She searched her closet for an article of clothing that would hide her bruise. The temperature was rapidly approaching 80 degrees outside leaving the option of a turtleneck out. She decided on a high-collar button-down and slacks. It would only hide her wound from the side but it would have to do. There were no serious plans to do any interviews today. Any follow up questioning could be done by telephone.

On her way into the office it occurred to her how odd Devon was behaving. The last thing she had expected was for him to leave her last night, especially after his almost maniacal concern for her. However, that's exactly what he had done. In fact, he acted as if he couldn't get away from her fast enough. Just thinking about it brought back the frustration from the night before.

He had taken her home, called the police and then turned and carried her upstairs. That's when the real weirdness had begun.

"Take off your clothes." he said softly

She stood looking at him still in a state of shocked denial over the horror of the past few hours.

He seemed to understand and began to slowly undress her himself. His fingers deftly negotiated the buttons on her blouse, unsnapped her bra with an expert snap of his fingers. He removed her pants going down on one knee to help her release each leg before standing, looking at her clad in only a skimpy pair of underwear. She remembered how silly she had felt as a single tear slipped from her eye. He was there then, quickly in one step steadying her, his big hand on her small waist, one finger wiping away the tear with his other.

She didn't understand the look in his eyes as his finger trailed down along the track of the tear to her neck. He always seemed so angry with her. She couldn't argue or explain. Let him be mad! His attention remained in that area a long time, eyes searching, fingers prodding. She flinched and before she was aware of what was happening, he had swept her up and was laying her on the bed. She remembered his hands on her. Asking her how each place he touched felt. It had taken her more than a few distracted moments to realize what he was doing. She was crushed when the realization struck her. He didn't want her; he was just making sure she wasn't broken.

She shivered, remembering. Then he'd left, only after being assured a police car would drive by every hour. He had been concerned but impersonal, almost cold. She always expected Devon to drift away from any personal involvement. She just hadn't expected it would be so soon. Charlie's entire body hurt from the obvious rejection. Knowing the more time that passed the more the hurt would turn to anger gave her hope. She needed that now. Needed the anger to cloud her other raging emotions.

In the following weeks she would be seeing Nick Devon every day. She would have to move past these feelings or move on.

The first person she saw when she arrived at work was a uniformed police officer. He was sitting in a chair in the lobby, drinking from a large Styrofoam cup. When he saw her, he waved. She walked over and the officer stood. He was short, 5'7, and stocky. His hair was dark and cut into a buzzed flattop.

"Ms. Morgan? Ms. Charlene Morgan?" he inquired.

"Yes." she said.

"Hello, I'm Officer Stan Mackey." he said as he pulled out a chair. "Have a seat. Detective O'Brien sent me over to take your statement."

"My statement?"

"Yes." he said. "About the attack last night." He motioned to her throat. "Did he do that?"

Charlie's hand came up and touched the bruised area. She flinched. "Yes."

"Can you tell me what happened?" Officer Mackey pulled out a small notepad and pen.

"I can't tell you much I'm afraid. He grabbed me from behind and pushed me out the door. That's when my boss, Nicholas Devon, showed up."

"You were inside when the attack began?" He scribbled something on his note pad.

"Yes. I was in my office finishing up some story ideas. I noticed it was getting late, so I packed up. When I was leaving my office, I thought I heard something.

"I dismissed it, thinking I was hearing things. As I opened the front door, he hit me from behind." Talking about it so soon was bringing it all back.

The officer looked confused. "You were unlocking the front door? How many people have keys?"

"Only three, the head writer, the editor-in-chief, and the lobby receptionist. She's the first to get here in the morning, so she lets the cleaning staff in."

"So the key you had?" he asked taking more notes.

"Oh. The head writer gave me his key. I was working late so he said I could drop it by his office today."

"He didn't need his key?" , raising an eyebrow.

"I haven't been here that long but I've never seen Garrett Quinlan show up on time." She smiled.

"Okay, so how many people knew you were working late?"

"Um... let's see." she said, trying to remember all of the people she'd spoken to that evening. "Garrett, Angie, the lobby receptionist, and Betty, Devon's secretary. So three as far as I know."

"Okay" he looked at his notes. "So, as far as you knew, you were alone in the building. However, the person that attacked you did so from inside. In addition, the door was locked, only three other people knew you were working late, correct?"

"Correct." she nodded.

"Is there anything else? Anything out of the ordinary that you can remember?"

"No. It's all a little blurry. It happened so fast."

"I understand. If you think of anything else, anything at all, you can call the station." He handed her a card.

"Thank you, Officer Mackey." She stood and shook his hand.

As he left, Charlie remembered something she hadn't had time to follow up on earlier. She walked over to the reception desk.

"Hey Angie. How are you today?" Charlie asked trying to sound light.

"I'm good." the dark haired woman behind the counter replied while staring at Charlie's throat.

"Angie." Charlie said, "I was wondering if you could help me with something."

"Sure Ms. Morgan. What do you need?"

"Do you know if there's an employee here by the name of Mike Mackenzie?"

"Mike Mackenzie? Doesn't sound familiar. I could check but I know everyone here."

"Great. I'd appreciate it if you could."

"I'll get right on it. Personnel has a list of all employees. I'll check with them."

By the time Charlie had turned on her computer and sat at her desk her telephone rang. It was Angie.

Mike Mackenzie was not currently, nor had he ever been, employed by The Post.

# CHAPTER 38

The bike path that led around the Cherry Creek Dam was teeming. People came out of their homes today to enjoy the exhilarating weather. Those who enjoyed the faster pace peddled by on the right. Charlie's legs pumped, her muscles screaming as she ran. She hadn't exercised since she arrived in Denver, three weeks ago and her body was telling her it had been too long. Underneath her sweatshirt and jogging shorts she could feel the sweat slowly soaking her clothing.

She reached up and brushed away a drop of sweat before it fell into her eyes. This morning as she'd left the house, the temperature was a chilly 55 degrees. In forty minutes it had risen drastically to a warm 75. Charlie reached into her hip pack and pulled out her water bottle. She opened it and drank, her legs still propelling her forward. She had two miles to go and she'd be back where she started.

Regardless of the heat and the burning in her muscles, she felt good. Exercise, no matter how strenuous, always gave her energy. It made her feel alive.

That's what she needed most, to feel alive. Amid all the craziness, having to deal with Devon was killing her. She still couldn't wrap her mind around how quickly he'd dropped her. Initially she'd convinced herself that he'd just been busy. Then she made excuses for him, like maybe he was overwhelmed with work or he was avoiding her to give her time.

*'Time for what?'* She didn't know. Finally, after her attack, she had expected the inevitable. He had his fun and moved on.

Her feet slammed against the pavement faster, her anger at Devon propelling her forward, her breath coming quick in great bursts, her arms pumping as she sped by the joggers on her left.

She was so immersed in her anger-induced adrenaline rush that she failed to notice the woman running beside her, desperately trying to keep pace with Charlie, while trying to appear casual. Finally, the woman gave up and loudly called:

"Charlene Morgan?"

Charlie stumbled, caught herself, and slowed her pace enough to look at the woman running beside her. She gaped at her in shocked disbelief. The blonde hair peeking from beneath the baseball cap. The bright blue eyes doing nothing to conceal her identity.

"Please don't stop running." Mary Fagon huffed the request, still keeping pace with Charlie. "There are people watching you."

Charlie continued her run, slowing her pace to a slow jog. She was winded from her sprint, the shock of seeing Mary and desperately wanted to stop and fall in the grass lining the path.

Instead she complied with Mary's request. She reached into her bag, grabbed her water and dumped all that remained on her head. The chilled water cooled her down significantly.

She kept her eyes forward and asked, "Where have you been? Don't you know your family is frantic?"

"It's a long story, one I'll be happy to share." Mary wheezed, trying to catch her breath. "But I'll never get through it this way. Where can we go that's private?"

"I think a crowd is better. The reservoir is around the next bend."

"O.K." Mary said still gasping for breath. "I'll find you." She dropped back quickly.

Charlie was stricken. The woman that caused all of this mess had just contacted her. She could be in incredible danger. She tried to keep a steady pace, appearing as if nothing changed.

She turned the corner and headed toward the reservoir. The crowd became dense. She maneuvered her way through heading toward the restrooms. She slowed her pace to a walk and entered the women's restroom. Mothers ushered their children out of the stalls and washed their hands, preparing for a day of sun and frolic.

She waited as a small child finished and moved to the sink. She splashed water on her overheated cheeks and refilled her water bottle.

Exiting the restroom, Charlie found a large tree at the edge of a playground and sat, leaning her back against the trunk. Its shade provided a prime spot for her; not too hot and with an excellent view of her surroundings.

Charlie watched, still astounded by these bizarre circumstances as Mary approached, casually walking through the playground. She made no eye contact. Her posture was slightly hunched. She wore a pair of khaki shorts and a tank top. Her blonde hair was tucked into a baseball cap pulled low, shielding her eyes, thin wisps falling to frame her face. It was obvious to Charlie that Mary had reverted to her former self, maybe in hopes of throwing off anyone who was looking for a the pictured missing woman.

Even in her state of casual dress, she was stunning. She came forward and sat beside Charlie. Mary leaned her head back on the tree trunk and closed her eyes. Her chest rose and fell rapidly, the only sign that she was not entirely relaxed.

Charlie wished she were more prepared. Her recorder would come in handy about now. Without preamble Charlie asked, "Did you kill your sister?"

Mary gasped, her head snapped toward Charlie. She quickly looked away resuming her previous posture. "No, I didn't. You're in even more danger than I thought. How long have you known?"

"Not long. I wasn't sure until now. How did you manage such a drastic transformation?" Charlie asked.

"Easy. I went to a salon and I took out my contacts. Does anyone realize that you know yet?"

"I was attacked recently," Charlie announced. "Because of your story. My attacker told me I'd been warned, but it was too late. I think he was going to kill me."

"Oh, no." Again she glanced at Charlie. "But you're still alive." She smiled weakly.

"Tell me why I'm in danger." Charlie demanded.

Mary took a steadying breath. "Powerful people have been looking for me for years. Stupid... I was never safe. I was just biding my time."

"So you ran away?"

"No!" she wailed. "I would never leave my babies."

Charlie was confused. "Tell me." She waited.

Mary closed her eyes and began speaking. Her voice held no emotion as if the entire trauma belonged to some other unfortunate soul. Charlie could tell she had been numbed by it all.

"Two years ago I began an affair. I knew that at the time it was wrong. Life was so good with Tony. My girls were happy and thriving."

Guilt shadowed her troubled face. "Tony was making good money and everything was perfect, too perfect. That was the problem. I was bored."

She bowed her head and then looked at Charlie determined to tell it all. "I met Carl Vail at a company picnic. He was so sweet, and he paid attention to me. It had been so long. Tony loved me, I knew that. But he had gotten comfortable, started taking advantage of me. Not in a bad way, just little things. We never went out anymore and sex... well let's just say I was spending more and more time alone. Anyway, when Carl started flirting with me..." She paused, sighing softly. "We started spending more and more time together. Things began to get more serious. I had never spoken about my past. Not even to Tony. I needed to talk to someone. Carl seemed like a good choice at the time. I told him everything. Not all at once but over time, six months maybe."

Again Charlie could see the shame. She wanted to assure Mary that she understood. She didn't. She knew any interruption would be a mistake.

Mary continued, unabated "He was a great listener. He was always reassuring, so kind. Then I found out I was pregnant. I knew it was Carl's because after Beka was born Tony had a vasectomy.

I went to Carl and told him. He dumped me on the spot. He denied the baby was his. It was like I was talking to a different person. He said if I tried to say the baby was his, he'd tell Tony about my past."

Charlie listened as Mary's voice trailed off; the pieces were falling into place. She waited patiently. When Mary resumed speaking, her voice had changed slightly. It had a soft quality.

"I went to Tony. I told him everything. We cried together all night. He forgave me. I'm still in awe of his goodness. I fell in love with him again that night. I never contacted Carl again. We avoided all company events and eventually life returned to normal. I gave birth to Kenny. Tony loved Kenny from the moment he was born. He is Kenny's father in every way that matters. I was so nervous that Carl would show up one day. I tried not to think about it. I kept Kenny with me all the time. I was almost obsessive about it. Then one day it happened. I was home with the kids. We were watching 'Blues Clues' on television. Carl called and said to come meet him right then. I was so frightened. I wanted him to just leave me alone."

Her voice cracked. "I went to meet him. I knew I should call Tony but I didn't know what he would do. Carl was so angry, so I went. When I got there he hit me hard enough to knock me out.

When I came to, I was tied up. He threatened to hurt Kenny if I didn't give him the names and telephone numbers of the people looking for me. I was so frightened that I told him what he wanted to know." Her face paled. "He was going to sell me back to them."

Charlie looked at Mary and felt saddened by what she'd heard. It was obvious she loved her children. To be threatened that way was unthinkable.

"How did you escape from Vail?" Charlie asked.

"One night he left and never came back. He was keeping me in his house. I managed to get free and run. I read in the paper the next day that he had been murdered. I freaked! I knew that they had come to get me. I couldn't go home. I wouldn't put Tony and the kids in that kind of danger, so I hid."

She reached out and grabbed Charlie's hand. "I need your help, please." Her eyes were pleading.

"What can I do?" Charlie asked. She wanted to help, but she didn't understand how she could.

"I read the story you wrote about me. The only way to get out of this is to expose my past. Let me tell you my story. It may be the only way to save my life. Please?" she beseeched Charlie.

Charlie stood, stretching as she spoke, reaching down and grabbing each ankle. "Go to my home. There's a small-gated area in front. No one will see you there. I'll run for a little longer, eat lunch and then I'll go home."

She started to give Mary her address.

"I know where you live," she interrupted Charlie. "I've been there." Mary turned and walked away without explaining.

For the third time in as many days, Charlie was told that she was being watched. It was unsettling even when this time it was so benign. She finished stretching and started jogging toward her car. At the moment she was relieved she had parked nearby. Still, it seemed to take forever before she reached it and managed to arrive in her neighborhood. A block from her house, Charlie stopped at a small café. She ordered too much food, intending to take some home; she lingered awhile over coffee, then paid the check and left.

When she arrived home, she took her time getting out of her car. Not looking around, she headed straight to her front gate, opened it, moved through and closed and locked it behind her. Mary was there sitting in the corner of the fence and front walk. She stood quickly and followed Charlie into the house. Once inside, Charlie placed the leftover food on the dining table and checked the back door to make sure it was locked.

Charlie sat at the table and watched as Mary ate the salad from the restaurant. When Mary finished, she put her plate in the sink and stood without moving. She seemed unsure of what to do next.

Charlie took the initiative. She pressed a button on her digital recorder and sat at the table. "You can start anytime you like." She waited as Mary also took a seat at the table.

She began her story, her face set and serious.

"I was born Victoria Lynn Ashley, an identical twin. My sister was Veronica Jean Ashley. I had a great child-hood. My parents were very wealthy. I grew up in a small coastal town in Massachusetts. My family was and still is very well known. William and Drucilla Ashley. I'm sure you've heard of the Claymores?"

Charlie nodded.

Mary smiled. "Everyone has. That's my mother's family. She was also a twin. It's very rare, you know, two sets of identical twins in consecutive generations.

"They were Drucilla and Cordellia Claymore. When they were growing up they were the talk of the town." She smiled tightly.

"Cordellia was the wild one. She was always getting my mom into trouble. Anyway, Cordellia apparently went too far and was cut off by her father. He left everything in his will to my mother. Soon after being disowned, Cordellia disappeared. My mother never spoke of her sister; we didn't even know she was a twin until we were almost teenagers. People in town eventually told Veronica and me the whole story. We were shocked, of course, but we understood. My parents never spoke of personal things. In my family, if you had a problem you saw a shrink or you dealt with it. You didn't whine about it to your family. Except with Veronica and I. We were close. We told each other everything. When we were 18, we went away to college. Veronica got a scholarship to N.Y.U. She was brilliant, she wanted to be a doctor." Her eyes welled up with tears, then brushed them away.

She seemed to need to steel herself for the next part of her story. She stood and went to the sink splashed water on her face and continued. Her back remained to Charlie. "It was our senior year in college and we decided to come home for Christmas and surprise our parents. When we arrived home we swore the staff to secrecy. We wanted it to be a surprise. They were out to some fundraiser so we went to our rooms to sleep, figuring they'd be home too late for the surprise to work well.

Anyway, Veronica went to sleep right away. I couldn't sleep so I decided to take a walk on the grounds. When I got back in the house, I heard voices coming from the study. I recognized my parents' voices. They were arguing. I decided to forget it and stick with the original plan when I heard something that stopped me cold.

My father was yelling at my mother. He said, 'Damn it, Cordellia! If anyone ever finds out we killed her, you'll go down with me!'

"Then I heard a loud slap. I think she hit him. I've had years to replay the scene in my head and it's almost as if I can see them. Then I heard her say, 'I'm sorry William, but you need to calm down. If the servants hear us...' Then I heard them go over what they had done, promising never to talk about it again. They were just standing there in my mother's house discussing a murder! I was so shocked I turned to run and knocked over a vase. It crashed to the floor. I ran out and I just kept running."

She turned to face Charlie; tears were streaming down her face. "I left Veronica there! She must have heard the crash and woke up. They didn't know it was me. I guess they thought it was her."

She paused, rubbed her eyes, and took a deep steadying breath. "Later, I started walking back, not sure of what to do but knowing I had to do something. There were ambulances and police cars everywhere. People were gathering around the gates of my home. I walked towards the house in a trance.

"When I got close, I saw them loading a body into the back of a long black car. I knew it was Veronica! I felt like I had been killed. I wanted to die. But more than that, I wanted to kill them. They were standing and holding each other, acting as if they cared. They didn't see me. I turned and ran." She was visibly shaken.

Charlie couldn't believe what she heard. To clarify all she had just been told, she asked, "So your aunt and your father killed your mother. Your aunt took her place. Then when they thought Veronica found out, they killed her?"

Mary nodded, grief coloring her expression. "When I ran, they must have figured out their mistake, because they blamed me for her murder." She put her head in her hands. Her body shook, she was sobbing.

Charlie realized that Mary had never been able to properly grieve. In one night she had lost her entire family, and was now shedding some of that awful pain. After Mary had regained some composure, Charlie took her into the guestroom. They sat on the bed talking about Veronica. Charlie asked lots of questions, not for a story but to help Mary remember so that maybe she might put those memories away.

They talked well into the night. Spent from hours of alternately laughing and crying, Mary finally fell asleep. Charlie covered her with a blanket and turned off the light, went downstairs and poured herself a glass of red wine. Lying in bed sipping the merlot she hoped for no dreams tonight. Charlie didn't want to think, didn't want to feel; after everything she'd learned, she was exhausted. Yet sleep did not come quickly. The wine hadn't helped as much as she hoped and visions of what Mary went through kept her awake well into the morning hours.

## CHAPTER 39

Charlie gathered all of her cds and the digital device and placed them in her briefcase. She needed to get Mary out of her house quickly. She was frustrated. Not knowing anyone in the area gave her few resources. She needed to find a safe place for Mary; somewhere that she could lie low until the story came out. After that, Charlie wasn't sure what would happen. Mary was still wanted for murder, a nasty complication.

Unfortunately, there was very little proof that what she told Charlie was true. Bringing it out in the open would only cast doubt on Mary's guilt. What she needed was proof that Drucilla Ashley was really her twin sister, Cordellia. Another unfortunate situation; identical twins have the same DNA, so proving Mary's convoluted story might prove impossible.

Charlie needed to find proof, some indisputable knowledge about Drucilla that did not apply to her sister. That would be ideal. The chances that such a thing existed were slim to none. *'But,'* Charlie thought. *'There was always hope'.*

She grabbed her briefcase and threw it in the car. She got in the driver's side and turned the key, giving it a second before pulling out of the driveway. At the end of the block she turned right and drove three blocks, heading out of her neighborhood. It was another gorgeous day, so it wouldn't seem unusual when Charlie drove into a self-serve car wash.

The opening didn't face the road and so it provided a perfect hiding place. Charlie dropped coins into the wash cycle and hosed off her car, only catching the slightest glimpse of Mary as she opened the rear passenger-side door and climbed in. Charlie took her time rinsing her car. Returning to the driver's seat, she slowly drove out of the covered car wash. She picked up her cell phone and held it to her ear, pretending to talk on the phone, and began speaking to Mary. "Are you O.K.?"

"I'm fine." The voice came from the backseat floorboard.

"Did you have any trouble? Do you think anyone saw you?" She was worried that all of this may prove too much for Mary. A person could only be expected to take so much.

"No problem. Luckily most people are at work so I didn't see anyone. Where are we going?" Mary asked.

"I'm not sure yet. I have an idea but I have to make a phone call. How do you feel about bringing someone else into this scenario?"

"Who?"

"Well…" Charlie hedged. "He's a police detective."

"A police officer?" Mary sounded stricken.

"He's a friend…..kind of. Anyway I think he can help. We don't have a lot of choices."

"O.K." Mary conceded. "I guess I need all the help I can get."

Charlie was relieved; she'd expected more of a fight. She dialed O'Brien's number, hoping he was in his office. She could only drive around aimlessly for so long without attracting unwanted attention. Luck was with her.

"Terrence O'Brien here."

"Hello, O'Brien, it's Charlene Morgan."

"Hello, Ms. Morgan. What can I do for you? Any new information?"

"As a matter of fact," she said, nervous about how he would react to this newest development. "I have someone here who needs police protection. It's a long story, so don't ask many questions, I need a safe place to stash her; then I'll come to you and tell you everything." Charlie held her breath.

"Bring her in." he said.

She let out her breath, disappointed.

"I can't do that. It's too dangerous."

"Ms. Morgan, this is highly unusual." He was obviously exasperated.

"Look, O'Brien, She knows things, things that could get her killed. She witnessed a murder." she blurted.

There was a long pause. When he spoke, O'Brien's tone had changed. "Okay, Get on Interstate 70, take it west for about fifteen miles. When you get to Golden, take the highway 36 exit, follow that for 3 miles until you see the Washington street exit, get off, and go north. You getting all of this?"

Charlie grabbed a pen, jotted down the directions on a small notepad attached to her dashboard; the phone was nestled between her right shoulder and ear. "Yeah, go ahead."

"Take Washington to the second traffic light, go left. That should take you directly into the mountains. The road curves a lot. Drive slowly. You're a city girl," O'Brien continued, "I don't want to have to scrape you off the rocks. If you see anyone behind you, pull to the right and let them pass."

"This will help to insure you're not being followed. Follow that road 9.3 miles. Then turn right on Mountain Valley road. After about one mile, it forks. Go left. It's a dirt road. Two miles it forks again. Go left. The cabin is at the end of a long, tree-lined drive."

Charlie looked at her pad. This was going to take over an hour. It should give her ample time to see if someone was following. "Does anyone know about this place?" she asked, concerned.

"Just close friends. Don't worry, I'll send a uniform to meet you there." he assured her.

"Okay." Charlie said

"When you get there, drop her off and come straight back here. I want the entire story. You have 3 hours. That should be ample time." He didn't sound like he was in the mood to negotiate. So she didn't try.

"Fine. Okay, I'll see you then...O'Brien?

"Yes?"

"Thanks." she said, grateful for his help.

"Don't screw me around, Morgan. This had better be good." He disconnected.

Mary's voice came from the backseat. "Everything okay?"

Charlie sighed. "I sure hope so Mary. I've found a safe place for you to stay while we work this mess out."

"Well," Mary said, "I guess my life's in your hands."

Charlie hated how true that statement was.

# CHAPTER 40

The drive back to Denver proved more difficult than the one leaving the city. Traffic had multiplied in the hour and half that had passed. She felt sure that no one had followed her to the cabin. When she and Mary had arrived, a uniformed police officer was already there; just as O'Brien had promised.

Nervous about being left there, Mary had argued with Charlie about leaving. She felt that Charlie was in great danger and had begged her to stay. Charlie understood the other woman's anxiety. Still, O'Brien had held up his part of the bargain; it was her turn to do the same.

She arrived at the Denver police department thirty minutes late. When she walked inside O'Brien was standing at the front desk. He quickly ushered her into his office, turned to her and said, "I've put my ass on the line, Ms. Morgan. You'd better have something for me."

Charlie walked past him and sat down. "The woman I'm protecting is Mary Fagon."

"I assumed as much. Where has she been?" he asked flatly

"Vail kidnapped her." she answered.

He looked confused. "Carl Vail has been dead for over a week. Where's she been since then?"

"Hiding. She thinks her family is in danger. I agree with her."

"Why?"

"Mary Fagon isn't who you think she is."

His eyes squinted. "Who is she?"

"Victoria Ashley."

"Victoria Ashley. Who is Victoria Ashley?" he asked, exasperation evident in his entire demeanor.

"Do you remember the twin murder, the case in Massachusetts? Veronica Ashley was presumably murdered by her identical twin?"

"This woman I'm helping is a murderer?" He looked stricken.

"No, I don't believe she is. That's what I need you to help me prove." She heard the desperation in her voice.

His cheeks reddened. "You must be joking. You want me to aid and abet a murderer?" His voice escalated, "I'm a detective. I could lose my job, not to mention go to prison."

"Just hear her out." She begged, "Once you hear what she has to say, I think you'll want to help."

"I don't have time to listen to her. You tell me." He walked behind his desk opened a drawer and pulled out a piece of paper.

"I just think she could make you understand..." she began, and then stopped, startled by his booming voice.

"Enough!" he shouted, slamming the paper down on the desk. "Look!"

Charlie stood and leaned closer. It wasn't a piece of paper; it was a forensic photograph. A man lying on his back on a gurney, fluorescent lights turning his skin a pale shade of green. His mouth was open wide in a silent scream of terror, dried blood filled the opening and overflowed covering his lower jaw and part of his neck.

Charlie stumbled back. She screamed. "Oh my God!"

"Do you know him?" he demanded an answer.

"Yes... Oh God, what's happening? I spoke to him a few days ago. His name is Jonathan Collins. He was Anthony Fagon's friend. They worked together." Her body was shaking, the words tumbling out.

"We know who he was." He dropped a slip of paper, contained in a plastic bag on the desk. "This was clutched in his hand."

Charlie stared at the paper in shock. Written in bold letters was the message: "Charlene Morgan, STOP TALKING!" She felt bile rise in her throat.

"They cut out his tongue." he said matter-of-factly. "Someone is out there killing people and from this piece of evidence, you're next. Start talking!"

"We have to get to Mary." Charlie said frantically. "She's in danger. Whoever is doing this wants to shut me up because of her."

"Why? How much do you know?"

"Victoria didn't kill her sister. Her parents did it to cover up the murder of her mother. It's crazy, I know, but she needs help."

Charlie knew she wasn't making any sense. She needed him to hear the story from Mary. She felt like they were running out of time.

"What did Jonathan Collins have to do with all of this?"

"Nothing. I spoke to him the other day. Just basic stuff about Mr. Fagon, He didn't seem to know anything about Mary."

O'Brien looked thoughtful. "That means that the killer is targeting the people you talk to, whether they know anything or not."

Charlie nodded slowly. "From what I gather, the only one who did know anything about Mary's past was Vail."

O'Brien looked doubtful. "What about Fagon? Surely she told her husband?"

"No." Charlie insisted. "She didn't. She kept it quiet for years. She only told Vail after they had an affair."

"So now the only people left who know anything are you and Mary Fagon?" he asked pointedly.

Charlie paled visibly. "Yes."

"You've told no one about this?" he stared at her intently.

"No." she assured him. A rope was tying itself in intricate knots inside her gut.

# CHAPTER 41

Detective O'Brien obviously had doubts. "What about Nick Devon?" he asked.

"No. He doesn't know anything."

"How well do you know him?"

"Who?" She was distracted by the question.

"Devon."

"Pretty well, I guess." Her answer was vague.

"Did he assign you this story?"

"Yes."

"You haven't updated him on your progress?"

"Sure. Basically, I just learned all the details recently."

"He hasn't pushed you for more information?" he pushed.

"No. What are you getting at, O'Brien?" She wanted him to stop hedging.

"I'm wondering why a hard-nosed news guy like Nick Devon hasn't been murdered. I'm also wondering why, when he saw you getting in over your head, didn't he reassign the story?"

"I'm not in over my head." Charlie said defensively.

O'Brien went on, "I'm also concerned about the fact that every time you were in danger, there he was. Don't you find that strange?"

"No!" She snapped. "He's protective! That's all!"

"Did he tell you why he just happened to be there when you were attacked?" he said bluntly.

Angrily she replied. "I didn't ask. I was too busy being grateful. He saved my life."

He waved her off. "Sure. But why was he there?"

"I don't know!" she yelled.

"Okay, skip it. What about Vail's murder? How did Devon just happen to show up there?"

"The answering machine. I forgot to turn it off. He listened to the message and heard where I was going." she said.

"Really?" he probed further. "Why would he do that?"

"He said he wondered why I was rushing out of the office so quickly." It sounded lame, even as she was saying it.

O'Brien saw the doubt on her face. "Are you sure he didn't follow you?"

"Yes, I'm sure. He didn't show up until after Vail was killed."

"How do you know that?" he demanded to know.

"I told you! He listened to the message."

"You're sure you didn't turn off the machine?" He was pushing her toward something he obviously didn't want to say.

Charlie was frustrated and scared. Her subconscious was trying to tell her something. She closed her eyes and tried to remember that night. The rain pounding on the roof, she wanted to go home. The telephone had rang. She'd picked it up late. She'd asked the person on the other line to hold on. The machine had completed; she'd heard a loud beep. She remembered reaching down and pressing the button. She replayed it again in slow motion. She could see it now she had turned the machine off before anything was discussed. There was no way Devon could have heard that conversation. She slumped in her chair.

"Oh, no." she croaked.

"Do you remember something?" he asked, knowing she had.

Shuddering with her new knowledge she said, "He lied to me."

"Is there anything else? Anything strange about his behavior?" he probed.

It all came rushing back, his showing up when she was in danger, never asking too many questions about the story. Why hadn't he reassigned it? After all, there were more qualified investigative reporters. Then the description of the man who'd questioned Tarrin came back to her. It had to have been Devon. Was he reading her files? Had he known about Victoria? She'd left her computer on her desk repeatedly turned on with everything right there for anyone to see. She wanted to scream.

*'Please!'* she thought, *'Not Devon! What possible motive could he have?'* Charlie was baffled.

"Even if he's been lying, what does that mean? He doesn't know Mary. Why would he try and hurt her?" Charlie queried.

"We don't know that. Maybe he does know her. Maybe he's been setting you up. I don't know, but I'm going to find out."

"How?" she said softly, afraid of the answer.

"We'll ask him." he stated. "Call him. Tell him you've blown the story wide open. Get him to meet you at the cabin. If he shows up with any evil intentions, we'll get him. If not," he shrugged, "At least we'll find out why he's lying."

Charlie hated the idea of setting Devon up. She loved him. Even with her doubts, she felt that emotion overwhelming her. She knew Devon had been the one who had questioned Tarrin but she'd pushed it to the back of her mind. She had intended to confront him. However, she hadn't. Instead she had been blinded by emotion and she'd slipped. Even now, she wanted to go to him, beg him to explain. It has to be some huge misunderstanding.

O'Brien interrupted her thoughts. "I've known Nick Devon for a long time. I've become quite friendly with him in fact. I understand how you feel. But," he paused dramatically. "He's always struck me as someone with a shady past."

"I don't know." she hedged, "I don't feel comfortable setting him up."

"I could have him arrested." he suggested. "Then your hands are clean."

"No!" she said emphatically. "Okay, okay, fine, I'll do it." She felt forlorn. She knew it might be disastrous but she had no choice. If Devon was involved, she had to know.

"I'll go now." she said. "I'll go. Just go to Mary and hear her story. I'll meet you there."

"Good." he said. "Call him. Then go straight to the cabin. I can't afford to have this leak. If word gets out about what I'm doing, I'm finished.

When I get to the cabin, I'll send Granby home." he said, referring to the officer he'd assigned to help Mary.

"Do you think that's wise?" She was growing more concerned for Mary by the minute.

"The less people that know about this the better. In addition, it's hard to hide a police car. If Devon is up to something, better he thinks it's not a set up."

"Sure, I guess." Charlie stood on wobbly legs and walked out of O'Brien's office. She would go to her car and call Devon from her cell phone. Once there, she dialed Devon's number with trembling fingers. After trying for several minutes, she realized her attempts were futile. Devon wasn't answering. She tried his home, office, and cell. No answer. She tried to think of the quickest way to get a message to him. She dialed again.

A strong male voice answered. "Garrett Quinlan."

"Hello, Garrett. It's Charlene Morgan."

"Hey, what can I do for ya?" He sounded pleased to hear from her.

"I'm trying to locate Devon. Have you seen him?" she asked, trying to sound as normal as possible.

"Sure. He was in his office earlier. As a matter of fact, he asked me about you."

"Oh. Well, I need to get a message to him. It's urgent."

"Sounds like it. He went out about 15 minutes ago. Said he'd be back. What's up?"

"I have some information pertaining to my story. I need his help. Do you have a pen?"

"I'm a writer. Of course, I always have a pen." He chuckled.

She ignored his humor, in no mood to laugh. "Great, take down these directions. I need him to meet me as soon as possible."

She gave him directions, reading them from the ones she'd written earlier.

"Yep, got it." he said. "I'll let him know."

"Thanks, Garrett. As soon as you see him, okay?" She knew she sounded desperate.

"No problem. Hey, is everything good?" he asked, concerned.

"No." she said honestly, "Nothing could be further from the truth."

"Sounds dire. Anything else I can do?"

"No, but I appreciate your concern." She disconnected and stared at her telephone. *'Oh. Devon,'* she thought. *'What am I doing?'*

## CHAPTER 42

The road leading to the cabin was a long, dirt, rutted path reminiscent of the horse and buggy days. Tall trees lined the edges on both sides, bending in toward each other in some botany-related mating dance. Intertwining at the tops they created a canopy. The effect was eerie, yet beautiful.

The sun was descending, altering the sky from its earlier blistering blue to a more pleasant violet shade. The small patches of light showing through the trees created an almost otherworldly sight.

At any other time this would have been a fabulous place to be. Not now. He walked toward his destination, barely controlling his need to break into a run. His need to let his body act of its own accord and fly toward the cabin must be kept in check.

His muscles bunched, his heart pounded. Yet he kept control, somehow following his plan, being casual, acting as if his internal organs weren't all being pushed to maximum capacity. Control, that's what it had all come down to.

He could see the door to the cabin clearly now. His hand brushed against his Glock, nestled securely in its shoulder holster, reassuring him that it was still there, as if a spirit from another dimension could remove it without his knowledge.

He stopped for a moment to look for any signs of life. There were none. He stepped closer and strained to hear. This was it. He continued forward and knocked. The door opened. He recognized the man in the doorway immediately. "You? All this time it was you, working behind the scenes?" He was genuinely surprised.

O'Brien stepped back and allowed the man to step inside. O'Brien looked smug. He was sure he had the upper hand, and the man could see it clearly now. All the near misses, were suddenly explained, someone always one step behind him, picking up the slack.

"Chris, I presume?" said O'Brien

"You know who I am. Why don't we stop the games and get down to it? Where is she?"

"Oh, not so fast, Chris, my boy. I've been biding my time very carefully until now. Things are going to go according to my agenda." He was feeling superior; it was obvious in his tone and swagger. That was good with such cockiness a slip up would be imminent.

The man stepped forward, his eyes ablaze, his intentions clear. O'Brien's hand came up and for the first time the man saw the gun. It was pointed straight toward his heart.

O'Brien spoke, "Don't get all commando on me, boy. I've come prepared. I know what you're capable of. I've known for some time. I won't be letting my guard down. I have no problem shooting you in your cold-blooded heart. Although it would be such a shame to do it before I'm ready. There's still so much fun to be had."

"Fun? What are you talking about? Aren't we on the same team, working for the same people? What's going on, O'Brien?"

"You'll see soon enough. First, let's take care of the preliminaries. Slowly take out your weapon and place it on that table over there." He motioned to the small table. "Don't try anything or this will end now in a very unpleasant manner. Are we clear?"

"Sparkling." he growled, visualizing his fist smashing into O'Brien's face. He would bide his time until he could make that fantasy come true. He reached inside his coat and very carefully released the small strap safely containing the Glock. He gripped it between thumb and index finger and pulled it out. He dropped it on the table and then slid his hands into his pockets, leaned against the wall and waited. He looked relaxed. Nothing could be further from the truth. He was a finely tuned, deadly weapon, just waiting to engage.

"Good." O'Brien said. "Now let's get on with the show, shall we?"

"What makes you think I'll play?" His voice sounded resonant but calm.

"Oh, you'll play, pal-o'-mine, you'll play 'cause I've got the ace in the hole. I have her. You want her, don't you?"

"Yeah, I want her. Where is she?"

"She's here." He stepped back a few steps and placed his hand on a doorknob. He turned it and pushed, the door swung open.

Inside, sitting on a chair, duct tape over her mouth, was Charlie.

Her feet were taped at the ankles, as were her wrists. She was bound up tight and scared as hell. When she saw him her eyes widened and she screamed, although through the tape it sounded little more than a moan.

# CHAPTER 44

O'Brien motioned him to enter the room and as he did, he noticed another woman, bound identically to Charlie her back against the same wall. This woman was easily identifiable. Except for her blond hair and glittering blue eyes, she was Mary Fagon.

"What's the plan, O'Brien? It looks as if you succeeded where I failed. You got her. What do you want with the other one? You were hired for the same reason I was, to locate and bring home the daughter. What's with the change of plans?"

"I never took you for the naive type before." O'Brien said. "The assignment was to locate and destroy. But this nosey bitch got to her first and now she knows. She could ruin everything. And now she knows everything about you." He reached out and ripped the tape from Charlie's mouth. Her eyes watered but she didn't make a sound.

She looked up slowly, the steely gray of her eyes filled with hatred. "How could you?" she said, "I trusted you." She choked on her next words. "I loved you, Devon!"

For the blink of an eye, Devon's control slipped. His skin was burning, his mind racing. She loved him. What a horrible way to find out. To see her sensuous lips say those words in the past tense was almost enough to send him spiraling over the proverbial edge; but not quite. He regained control quickly and grinned, giving away nothing.

"Well sweetheart, nothing lasts forever." he said, sounding as if he couldn't have cared less about her. He turned to O'Brien. "What now? I assume you have some grand plan?"

"The plan is you all die, and I'm a hero. I like it; what do you think?"

"Clean. But why kill me?" he smirked, his eyebrows raising.

"Loose ends. Plus, I need someone to blame for their murders."

"Oh, I see, makes sense; but you've forgotten something." Devon said matter-of-factly.

"Oh yeah?" O'Brien queried. "And just what would that be?"

"Motive. Why would I kill Charlie, not to mention her?" Devon said, pointing to Mary. "Nick Devon, Editor pillar of the community, doesn't even know her."

O'Brien shook his head. "What you don't seem to understand is they won't care. You were found here with two dead bodies. Before I could make any sense of the situation, you tried to take me out. I'm a respected officer of the law. Case closed."

Devon finished O'Brien's thought. "And of course you take me out, saving the day."

"Precisely." O'Brien smiled a big toothy grin. "I knew you were bright. Now let's get on with it. You choose. Which one first? I'll let you think about that while I prepare the crime scene. Come with me, Chris. Let's go get your gun." They walked into the front room where O'Brien picked up Devon's gun, all the while, keeping his weapon leveled at Devon.

"Okay It's party time. Sit down on the bed, you get to watch."

Devon sat. His plan was made. While O'Brien had been speaking, he was calculating his odds. He had taken in every aspect of his surroundings and he was ready. As long as everything went according to plan, they would all get out of this alive. Just as he was ready to spring, Charlie spoke, stopping him.

"Why?" she was looking at O'Brien. "What possible reason could you have for doing this?"

"The time for questions is over. I'm truly sorry I have to kill you, Ms. Morgan. I've liked you since the first time I met you. You're savvy, with good instincts. If you remember, I tried to get you to let this go; but," He paused, shrugged, and said, "a dog with a bone."

"You're going to kill me and not even tell me why?" she asked, hoping to stall the inevitable.

Devon breathed a sigh of relief. He could tell by the look on O'Brien's face that his ego had gotten the better of him. He was going to brag, giving Devon just the extra time he needed to carry out his plan.

O'Brien began pacing. "Fine. The least I could do is grant a dying woman her last wish. I did it for the money."

"Money? You're going to kill innocent people for money? But you're a cop! You've been a detective for years!"

O'Brien laughed. "My dear child, you don't think money is a good reason for murder? Let me assure you that it's the very best reason. In addition, after you and this little slut are dead, I am going to have loads of it. If Chris here had stayed on board, he'd be in the same boat."

Charlie turned toward Devon. "Why does he keep calling you that?"

O'Brien chose to answer her, "Chris is his code name. Don't you get it, Saint Nicholas, Chris Kringle? I think its brilliant. Your sweetheart is a hired killer who thinks he's Santa Claus." He laughed again.

"But that man who killed Mr. Vail was English, I heard him speak. There has to be some mistake." Her eyes begged Devon to deny the accusations. "Please?" she said, hoping there was some mistake.

"Go ahead," O'Brien instructed Devon. "Tell her the truth. Am I lying? Are you just some innocent bystander that somehow got caught up in all of this?"

Devon was angry, seething with hatred for O'Brien. He ached for her as he did the only thing he could do under the circumstances. He became Chris. The lids of his eyes closed slightly, his chin dropped, and his jaw clenched. It all happened very quickly, but the change was evident. Charlie gasped. When he spoke, the accent was in place, the charade complete. "The last thing anyone could accuse me of is innocence. Vail needed offing. It's as simple as that."

O'Brien smiled at Charlie. "I told you to watch out for him. Can't you see, I've always had your best interests at heart?"

Charlie stared. A stream of tears slipped silently down her cheeks. She turned her head, trying to block them from seeing her pain. Her heart was breaking. She could not believe this was the same man she loved. She had to know the truth.

Charlie turned to O'Brien. "Allow me die with some peace. If all this is true, why would you kill the assassin working for the same people you work for?" As she asked, the last shred of hope ebbed away.

# CHAPTER 45

"Mary Fagon is really Victoria Ashley, but you already know that. I've been looking for her for a long time. Spending all my time and energy. I started working for her father the year she disappeared. I was promised lots of money to find her. I couldn't find a thing for years. She was good; she had completely disappeared. Then I find her and she's slutting around with Vail. That was her downfall."

He walked over to Mary and placed his hand on her cheek. She flinched. He leaned down and looked into her eyes. Devon and Charlie both watched in horror as he placed the gun under her chin.

"If you hadn't been slutting around, you might have gotten away with it, poor girl. You picked the wrong guy to tell your secrets to."

Mary began to cry, her body shaking. O'Brien stood, backed away from Mary, and swung the gun around towards Devon.

"I found her. That fool Vail contacted the family. I traced the calls. I found her. ME!" He screamed this last.

"Then they call him," he pointed at Devon accusingly. "And I become second fiddle. I knew Devon's background but I couldn't be sure he was the elusive Chris. So, I set a trap. Looks like it worked. I'll save the day, collect the money, and then when it's all blown over, I retire. No need to wait for my pension and stupid gold watch."

"Sounds like you've really got it all worked out." said Devon. "What makes you think William Ashley won't turn on you? He has a lot to cover up; you're a loose end."

O'Brien reached into the collar of his shirt. He withdrew a small key attached to a chain. "Insurance, my boy, insurance. This key opens a safety deposit box containing all the details of his crimes, audio taped telephone conversations and documents. How do you think I became authorized to kill you?" He asked smugly

"These people are powerful, not to mention stinking rich. They liked having you on their payroll. I convinced them otherwise. After this mess goes away, I disappear with their money and all the proof of their crimes, insuring my long life." He sounded triumphant.

Charlie was still confused. "Why did you kill Tarrin and Jonathan Collins? Why not just Mary? Was it to keep your secret because they saw your face?"

Devon abruptly realized she was talking to him; she assumed he had killed those people. He could see it in her face; he felt cold inside, empty. Devon had spent years coming to terms with his past. He had never fully recovered from the guilt. His night with Charlie had started to change all that. The dreams were becoming less frequent. He mistakenly believed that having someone so good want him, care for him, he must be worth forgiving. That changed the moment she discovered his secret.

Now looking into her hate filled eyes, he knew he would always be that man. After working for the government for five years earning a reputation that surpassed all of his colleagues, he burnt out; suddenly it had all become too much. Now he was the guilty one again, the one not to be trusted, he was right back where he'd started. His gut twisted but he showed no reaction to the physical pain.

O'Brien broke his reverie. "You're giving him too much credit, Ms. Morgan. He was hired for his reputation. Ashley didn't know he had gone soft. The only reason he took the job was so Ashley wouldn't blow his cover. You see, they knew about him. That William Ashley is a ruthless bastard. What did they threaten you with exactly?"

Devon looked at Charlie. "I'm sure she doesn't care." he shrugged.

"I want to know!" O'Brien waved his gun. "We're all being honest here so tell me! Why did you come out of retirement?"

Charlie was holding her breath, wanting to hear his answer. He could see that she needed to know. It would have to wait.

O'Brien moved closer to Devon, his anger clouding his judgment. Devon smiled; too late O'Brien realized his mistake.

Devon's right fist came up hard in a shattering blow, connecting with the underside of O'Brien's chin. His head snapped back. Losing his balance he stumbled. Devon flew at him, his leg coming up and then slicing down in an axe kick, knocking the gun from O'Brien's hand. By the time O'Brien's body hit the floor with a resounding thump, Devon had retrieved the gun.

Devon knelt beside O'Brien. Lifting the gun in a wide arc he brought it down swiftly. Slamming the butt into the side of his skull effectively, knocking him unconscious. O'Brien's body went limp.

Devon collected the second gun from O'Brien's still form; he slipped it into his waistband and slid the Glock into its holster.

He bent down, lifted his pant leg and withdrew the knife strapped to his leg. He walked to Mary and cut the tape, releasing her ankles and wrists. As she pulled the tape from her own mouth, she was obviously overwhelmed. Still unsure of Devon, she said nothing. He helped her over to the bed where she sat, still shaking. She began to rub her aching wrists and ankles to restore circulation.

Devon went back to O'Brien, bent down and yanked a chain from his neck. He slid the cabin key into the inside pocket of his jacket.

"Devon?" Charlie said in a voice barely above a whisper.

He turned and looked at her. "You have a choice to make, Morgan. Before I untie you, I need you to listen."

She opened her mouth to speak but no words emerged. She was confused. So much had happened in such a short span of time. She had questions. Unfortunately, she didn't know if she could handle the answers.

Devon knelt down in front of her. He leaned in close and said, "There's only one way out of this. If you work with me, I think I can end this with no more casualties. Can you trust me?" he asked.

"Trust?" she mumbled. He could see it would not be easy for her.

Then she laughed. It was an ugly sound, low in her throat. She felt betrayed with good reason. "Let's not use that word. I'll go along with your plan, but only because I want to live. I'll never trust you. You're a murderer." She practically spat the words at him and again he felt a twisting inside him. He could see she was angry and hurt. He only hoped someday she would understand and forgive.

He would wait. "Fine. For now, that will do. Is your car parked nearby?" he asked.

Charlie nodded.

"Good. I'll give you an address; I want you to go there. Take Mary with you. Stay put; I'll come for you when it's safe. Morgan, I want you to write the story. Reveal all the facts, everything."

Charlie, nodding, understood. Writing the story, telling the public, was the only way to save Mary.

"Okay," she said. "Untie me."

"In a minute. First I want to tell you…" He stopped and shook his head. "There's no time. I hope you give me the chance when this is over." He began cutting her ankles loose. "Take your laptop with you. I'll contact you. You can e-mail me the story as soon as it's done. Publishing it will be the final part of my plan."

Devon sliced through the tape on her left wrist but before she could lift her arm, he placed his hand over the same area that had just been released, holding her captive again. He stood, placed the knife in her hand held captive by his.

"When I leave, cut your other hand loose and leave here quickly. I'd do it for you but I need a head start. I can't have you following me." He reached into his jacket, retrieved a small card, and dropped it in her lap. She looked down. There was an address on it. She looked up again, directly into Devon's face. He had leaned close, his breath dusting her lips. She gasped.

He looked into her gray eyes and made a decision. He needed this, maybe more than he had ever needed anything. His mouth was on hers before she could draw a full breath. His lips were soft, the kiss wasn't. His tasted and felt the reserve in her as he pressed forward. Tasting, plunging, withdrawing only to plunge again. He was lost in her, consumed by her smell and taste, immersed in the texture of her. His hand pulled her hair, tilting her head back, allowing him more access to her mouth. He wanted to overcome her desire to hate him. He was taking her with him, her tongue now moving with his. It was a desperate moment for both. It was the last kiss of two people desperately in love but unwilling or unable to bend. It ended as abruptly as it had begun. He shook from the intensity of the moment then said in demanding tones "Be quick, Morgan. You don't have much time. He'll only be out a half an hour at best."

# CHAPTER 46

Charlie's eyes were glazed. At first she didn't seem to understand. Then it all came back. Clear. She started to shake with anger, appalled by it all, overwhelmed by her emotions. She took the knife and started cutting through the tape. When her arm was free she looked up. He was gone. She hadn't even heard him leave.

Ω

Charlie handed a printout of the story to Mary. It had taken three rewrites and several long conversations. Finally, she had something she was happy with, more than happy with in fact. It was good.

The facts of the case were extraordinary, the stuff of thriller movies. It contained everything; murder, kidnapping, adultery, all the makings of a good mystery.

She sipped her coffee and watched Mary as she read. Several times Mary's face changed, displaying emotions ranging from happiness to the depths of grief. When she'd finished, tears were streaming down her face. She sat the printout on the coffee table and her eyes met Charlie's. A weak smile curved her lips.

"Thank you Charlie. No matter how this plays out, people will know my story." She brushed her tears away. "More than anything, I don't want my children to grow up in the shadows of my tragic life."

"Don't worry Mary. I can see how much you love your children. With a mother like you, they'll have a strong foundation. Kids are stronger than we give them credit for."

Mary's eyes filled with gratitude. She smiled again. This time it lit up her entire face. Her natural beauty struck Charlie.

"What do you think Anthony will say when he sees you, now that you look quite different."

Mary looked stricken for a moment. "I hadn't thought of that. I'd probably call him to prepare him. Luckily, Tallon resembles me, so it shouldn't be too much of a shock. After all, he's been saying for years that I would look great as a blond."

"Do you think he's going to understand why you didn't confide in him?"

"If it were anyone but Tony, I'd be worried, but he's one of the kindest, most understanding men alive and if there's one thing I'm sure of it's that he loves me. I didn't know how much until Kenny was born."

Charlie felt a pang of regret. "Hold onto that love. It's very rare." She thought of Devon. Could she forgive him as easily? She knew she still loved him. Her anger had overshadowed her feelings temporarily.

She wondered what was keeping him so long. They had been staying in this apartment for five days and they had had no contact with the outside world. The apartment was in a small town just outside of Denver. When they arrived, they found a wonderfully comfortable completely stocked residence. It was obvious somebody spent quite a lot of time here.

Upon arriving, they realized they had only the clothes they were wearing. Fortunately, after searching the bedroom, they found a complete wardrobe. All men's clothing, all dark colors, but they would do. Both women wore oversized sweatpants and buttoned-down shirts the majority of their stay. They discovered a washer and dryer but had decided to have their clothing washed and fresh for the day they left. Not knowing when that would be, they made do with what was available.

The first two days of their self-imposed incarceration were spent getting to know one another. Charlie never had many girl friends growing up. Later she'd been too busy to cultivate any new ones. They shared their feelings about their current situation. That quickly escalated into things that are more personal. Mary explained that her first job was dancing at a small gentleman's club. She talked about how badly she'd just wanted to disappear.

Dancing had seemed like the perfect way to make money fast and lie low. She'd met Anthony Fagon when he dropped by her job to pick up money for his mother, who owned several other clubs around town. There had been an instant attraction.

Initially it terrified her; trust was something that no longer existed for Mary. But Anthony had been persistent, sending roses, showing up in the middle of her shifts. Finally Mary consented to a date. She described it as the greatest night of her life. She'd been so afraid of her feelings that she quit her job and hid out for over six months. Finally feeling stronger, she reapplied and was hired at a different location.

Not soon after, Anthony had rediscovered her. A romance had blossomed. He'd insisted she quit her job. He became a terrific husband and father. Mary told Charlie about the days her babies were born and during these conversations, they laughed more often than not. Charlie had never seen motherhood in such a wonderful light before.

In turn, Charlie told Mary about her childhood. She explained how growing up in a supportive home had given her such a strong foundation. She told her about her college days and her earlier experiences with Nick Devon. She was expressing her feelings aloud for the first time, her heart fluttering as she said the words. When she told Mary about their, recent night together, Mary gasped aloud and told Charlie how lucky she was.

Then seeing the look on Charlie's face, she realized the true depth of Charlie's pain. It was Mary's turn to listen and lend support as Charlie vented. She talked for hours explaining how they had come together only to have him distance himself. She'd cried heart wrenching sobs as she relived the last time she seen him. He'd been so cold. Mary tried to reassure her that it must have been an act for O'Brien sake. She didn't get far. The man she loved had lied to her. Mary hoped for Charlie's sake that Devon could mend the fences he'd torn down.

Mary sat with her back braced against the headboard, her legs were bent, arms wrapped around them, head resting against her knees. She felt drained. So much had happened, her life turned upside down because of one mistake. She wondered what it must be like for Charlie, a simple existence.

Mary looked at her new friend as she sat in a big chair at the end of the bed. They had been this way for hours, talking. So much had been said; yet she still felt as if there were more.

"Charlie?" Mary said.

Charlie's head turned to look at her. "Yeah," Charlie answered, "I'm still here, just thinking"

Mary could see that despite what she said she wasn't all there. Her mind was obviously elsewhere. She felt indebted to Charlie. She wanted to do something for her, needing to feel like she was giving something back.

"Charlie. I need you to listen to what I'm going to say. You may not feel like it has any merit. But everything I'm about to say I've learned from painful experience. So please try to really listen."

Charlie seemed to understand. She leaned forward slightly and nodded her head.

Mary took a deep breath. "When I was young, my mother told us to take responsibility for our actions. At the time I thought that she meant that we needed to accept our punishment for things we'd done wrong." She laughed remembering how naive she had been.

"Now I know exactly what she meant. Everything that we do, right or wrong, has consequences. Some are wonderful, others catastrophic. I remember the day Veronica and I decided to go home for Christmas. We were so happy. We laughed at the idea of surprising them. There was this moment, before we decided to go. That moment changed my life forever and it ended hers."

Her eyes clouded with unshed tears. She closed her eyes fighting them off. "If I could go back and change that moment...You see the problem, don't you?"

Charlie smiled sadly. "I think I do."

Mary went on, "Would I change it? I can't answer that, but I'm glad I'm not able to. In that moment I lost my best friend, my twin. But another thing happened in that moment. I set in motion a string of events that led me to Tony and my wonderful children. There's no love like the love you feel for your children. I feel guilty for saying it, but not even the love of a twin equals it."

Charlie sat forward. "How can you feel guilt about that? Don't you think Veronica would be happy you feel so deeply for your children?"

Mary lost the battle. Tears streamed down her face. "I know Veronica as well as I know myself. You're right she would understand. It still changes nothing. She's gone. So every time I experience happiness, I feel guilt, for all the happiness she will never feel. I know it's unhealthy and someday maybe I'll let it go. Not yet, I'm not ready yet. Someday with the love of my children and, if he'll ever forgive me, my husband, I'll get healthy again. That's when I'll say goodbye."

"You know," Charlie said. "When this is all over, you can tell the kids all about Veronica. She'll live on through your memories."

Mary smiled through her tears. "Yes, I'll do that. I'll tell them. I'll also tell them this." She looked pointedly at Charlie "Don't take this lightly. Realize that from your greatest moments of sorrow to your most profound happiness, every decision counts. Knowing this probably won't make a difference; you and I will move on from this, touched but not shattered. But, at some future time, when life is once again hinging on an event, we'll remember. Just think about this moment; it may make all the difference." She fell silent. hoping some of what she said would help; maybe not now, but someday.

Charlie moved and sat beside her. Mary gratefully accepted the comfort given so easily. As Charlie's arms surrounded her she rested her head on Charlie's shoulder and cried silent tears. She knew the waiting was almost over for her. She hoped the same was true for Charlie.

Ω

After three days together, they had become friends. Comfortable now, they embarked on more crucial information. They discussed her mother's murder, trying to determine when it may have taken place. Mary wasn't sure. She assumed it must have happened when she and her sister were young, before they possessed the knowledge of their mother's background.

She could remember a time when, at about the age of ten, their mother had become colder, spending less time with her children and more time involved in social activities. The sisters had noticed the change but had assumed that they weren't young enough anymore to require the care they had in the past. They had been there for each other so the change wasn't devastating.

Mary expressed that she would forever carry the guilt of those days, not realizing that someone had taken her mother's place. She felt cheated. Years later, she was grieving for a woman who had died two decades before.

Days passed and both women felt as if they knew each other well. The story complete, all they could do was to continue to wait. They busied themselves making lunch and chatting about Mary's children. They were in the kitchen preparing a meal when the telephone rang.

# CHAPTER 47

All activity immediately stopped and two sets of eyes stared at the telephone it as if it were a snake.

Slowly Charlie approached, picked up the handset and held it to her ear and listening silently.

Devon's voice seemed to caress her "Charlie? It's Devon."

"I know." Her heart was slamming against her chest.

"Turn on the television, CNN. I'll call back in thirty minutes." The line went dead. She replaced the telephone and walked to the television. Her adrenaline was working overtime as she turned it on and yelled "Mary! Get in here!" She watched as the screen blazed to life. Mary ran in the room as the anchor on the news began to speak.

*"We have a late breaking news bulletin. Just this afternoon three people were arrested on murder and kidnapping charges in locations ranging from Denver, Colorado to Massachusetts. All of the details have yet to be released. As of now this is what we know."*

The picture on the screen changed showing a handcuffed Terrance O'Brien being placed in a police car. His head was down but there was no mistaking who he was.

Charlie sat on the couch, her mouth drawn in a straight line as she watched. Mary was kneeling on the floor staring at the TV entranced. The TV anchors voice detailed his arrest.

*"Terrance O'Brien a well-respected Denver police detective was arrested on suspicion of three murders involving conspiracy and blackmail. His accomplices were also arrested on the small island of*

*Nantucket, Massachusetts in the involvement of these and several other deaths. As of now, we are also being told that Victoria Ashley is being sought for questioning. She may have vital information in the arrest of her parents Drucilla and William Ashley."*

A picture of Mary flashed on the screen. Mary covered her eyes and moaned. "Oh no! Tony is going to see this. I have to call him." she said wearily.

Charlie listened as the story ended.

*"Please stay tuned for further updates as they are received."*

Charlie looked at Mary. "It should be safe now. Call him."

Mary stood and walked to the bedroom and she shut the door. Charlie soon heard Mary's soft voice as she spoke to her husband for the first time in a month. She was still sitting on the couch staring at nothing when Mary came in holding the telephone. "It's Devon." She held the telephone up to Charlie.

Charlie took the handset and held it to her ear. "Hello?" she said.

"Hi. How are you holding up?" He sounded good. She had missed his voice.

"I'm okay. Better now. Are we safe?" She tried to sound upbeat but failed.

"Have you finished your story?"

"Yes." she said

"There's a fax machine in the bedroom. Fax it to my office now. It'll go in the morning edition."

"Okay." She cared less and less about her story by the minute.

Devon continued: "I need to bring Mary in. How is she?" He sounded so casual she wanted to scream.

Instead, she said, "As good as could be expected. She's been through a lot."

His voice changed. It became huskier. "I know. She's not the only one. How are you?"

Just talking to him was doing things to her body. She tried to focus. "Not great, but I'm alive. You know what they say... I guess I'm stronger."

"That was never your problem," he stated.

"I don't feel very strong right now." she admitted. He seemed to understand her veiled reference.

"Send the story, Morgan. I'll be there tonight. We'll talk. In the meantime, Garret is coming by to get Mary. After she gives her statement, she can go home."

Charlie was relieved. "I'll tell her."

"Morgan? I want to come by. Do you want me to?"

She took a deep breath, exhaled and answered. "Yes." She listened as the telephone went dead. She wasn't sure what would happen now but she desperately wanted to find out.

# CHAPTER 47

Mary had been thrilled by the news. Her conversation with her husband had gone well, and he just wanted her to come home. After that, he promised they would work everything else out.

Charlie hugged Mary and promised to keep in touch. Both women wanted to salvage the one good thing that had come out of this: their friendship. Now Mary was gone and Charlie sat alone at the dining table sipping her coffee. She changed into her clothing and spent the rest of the afternoon restoring the apartment to its original state.

All of the clothes that they had borrowed were now neatly returned to their appropriate drawers or hangers. The dishes were all done and the bed made. She even vacuumed and dusted. Now completely out of mindless chores to do, she sat waiting. When the doorbell rang, she was startled and nearly knocked over her coffee.

She walked toward the door as butterflies beat out the now familiar Cajun rhythm, their wings tickling her stomach lining. She opened the door.

Devon stood there looking uncomfortable. His hair was standing up in various places as if it had been professionally mussed. She was sure he had just spent a moment toweling it dry after a shower. He wore a black snug pullover that accented his broad chest and defined stomach. A pair of faded jeans hung from his lean hips. On his feet were snakeskin cowboy boots. Charlie drank him in with her eyes. She couldn't remember him ever looking better.

She stepped back without saying a word. He brushed past her, his arms behind his back, one hand gripping the other at the wrist. He stopped in the middle of the living room, turned, and faced her. He seemed ready for battle. The air was thick with tension. Charlie felt she needed to say something. Not knowing where to start she said, "Coffee?"

One corner of his mouth turned up. "Some things never change. No thanks, I'm fine."

She decided to dive right in. "Did you kill them?"

He didn't need her to clarify. "Only Vail."

Her heart sank. "O'Brien killed the others?"

"Yes. Hoping to scare you off."

"Why did you kill Vail?" She felt her resolve harden with the knowledge that he was a murderer. Hearing this from his own lips made it real.

He let out a long breath. "It was a mistake. I heard you. When he told me you were there...I slipped. I was sloppy. He saw my reaction and went for the gun. It was a deadly mistake." Devon was watching her closely, gauging her reaction. She tried to hide her emotions from him.

"So you're a hired killer?" she asked bluntly.

"I was, for the government. I'm retired." He was becoming more uncomfortable, his posture stiff, his expression stoic.

"I was there, Devon. It didn't sound like retirement." she accused. She felt him watch her as she walked toward the table, picked up her coffee and sat. Her legs wouldn't hold her much longer.

He turned toward her, his posture remaining the same, hands behind his back, feet slightly apart. "I worked very hard to have a normal life. Somehow, Ashley got a hold of my confidential file. He knew everything. All the details of my past. Every contract I was employed by our government to carry out. All he wanted was for me to find his daughter." He shrugged. "I went along. For a while I ran into one brick wall after another. Then you stumbled upon her."

"When you assigned me the story, you didn't know that Mary was Victoria?" The skepticism in her voice was ripping, she hoped he heard it.

"No." he said tightly. "I only discovered it when I saw the name 'Carl Vail' in your notes." He took a small step forward, seemed to think better of it, and stopped. "Shortly after Mary was kidnapped but before I had any information, a man named Carl Vail called Ashley. He threatened to kill Victoria if his demands weren't met. I saw the name on your notes. I was hoping to end it before you contacted him."

"You were going to end it? What do you mean? Kill him?" she accused. At this point she didn't care if she was being fair. He had lied to her at every turn.

"No, dammit! I just needed to find Victoria. He had her. I went there to question him."

"Then you heard me?" she asked.

He nodded.

"If I'd seen you that night, would you have killed me?" she whispered.

His eyes squinted, anger blazed there. "Not then, maybe now." came the terse whisper.

Her eyes widened, her coffee cup dropped from shaking fingers and spilled onto the carpet. He was on her in a second. His strong hands jerked her from her chair by her upper arms, pulling her forward. He looked down into her wide gray eyes.

"I would never hurt you. How can you look at me like that?" he demanded. His voice dropped. "You said you loved me."

She stepped away pulling from his grip. "Love isn't always the most powerful thing. Fear can be much more powerful." Charlie looked into his eyes, no longer filled with anger. There was pain.

"How can you be afraid of me?" he asked, tormented.

She realized that nothing else mattered to her but erasing his hurt. She lifted her hand and placed it on his cheek. He flinched.

"Are you afraid of me now?" she asked, stunned by his reaction.

"Yes," he said, in a dry voice. "You have the power to end me. Will you?" he asked.

"Please don't look at me that way." she pleaded

He took the step that bridged the gap between them and put his hand on her cheek, his thumb brushing her bottom lip "I've explained everything. I want you to trust me again. Ask me anything. I will tell you the truth. I'm so sorry, all I've ever done is try to protect you, please let me do that... Forever,"

She tried to understand his meaning. "Forever?" she mumbled.

"Morgan ...do you love me?" He put a finger to her lips. "Don't start arguing. Just answer the question."

She nodded " I think I always have."

He groaned and crushed her to him, burying his face in her hair. "Thank God." he said, "I thought you hated me."

She could feel his heart pounding in her ear. When he spoke again her knees gave way and Devon swept her into his arms. She had never heard sweeter words than these...

"I love you, Morgan!"

# CHAPTER 48

C harlie woke with a start. A fear raced through her. In the darkness she could hear Devon's deep breathing. She nudged him, trying to wake him, needing to have one last question answered. One question she had overlooked in her rush toward emotional fulfillment. Devon rolled until his face was inches from hers. His eyes opened. "Again? So soon? I think I may need a little more time to recharge."

Charlie laughed. "No. I barely had enough energy for last time." Devon grabbed her and rolled, pinning her beneath him. Small patches of light, illumination from the streetlights outside, broke up the darkness of the room. His face was inches from hers. She could just make out a devilish grin playing across his mouth.

He leaned forward and brushed his lips to hers in a feather light caress.

"Devon?" she murmured.

"Hmm?" He was obviously distracted.

"MMM." He began nibbling on her neck and ear-lobe.

"Devon!"

His head came up slowly, a look of innocence on his face. "Yeah?"

"I'm serious." she said. "I need to ask you about your file."

He lifted himself higher resting on his forearms. "My file?"

Exasperated now, she said, "Yes. You said William Ashley had your file. Are you going to stay retired or is someone else going to blackmail you? I can't keep going through this." The idea sent chills through her.

He looked unconcerned. "I got it back. It was the original. There are no more copies. I called my superiors. They've all been destroyed. 'Chris' no longer exists." He grinned. "Can I go back to what I was doing or are you going to scream in my ear again?"

Charlie put a hand on his chest, stilling him. "How'd you get it back?"

"What?" It was obvious that he was having trouble focusing.

"The file!" She rolled her eyes.

"Oh that. I blackmailed the attorney. He was my contact. In that little box of O'Brien's there were loads of papers incriminating McNeally. He would have gone to jail for a long time. Even trade. My file for his. He was more than happy to oblige." He looked at her mischievously. "Can I proceed with my seduction now?"

"I wish you would." she said, wrapping her arms around his neck. "I never want to leave this bed."

He kissed her neck. "I'd be happy to keep you here forever but unfortunately, I have to be home tomorrow."

"Why?" she said, frowning.

"My sister's coming to town. She's thinking about moving here."

"You have a sister?" Charlie was stunned.

"Twin sister. You're gonna love her. She's just like me."

Charlie moaned, "Are you kidding? There can't be that many twins in the world!" she was calculating the possibilities. "I mean really..."

"Shut up Charlene." he ordered. When she opened her mouth, he silenced her with a deep soul-racking kiss.

~~~~~

# Editor's Note

Samantha Shu's *Blood Line* is the prequel to her widely successful debut suspenseful story, *Whispered Dreams* (A-Argus Better Book Publishers, November 2008). Following are excerpts from Shu's best-selling novel of love, murder, danger ant thrills, *Whispered Dreams,* the second in her trilogy (*Blood Line; Whispered Dreams; Blood Thirsty*) of thrilling suspense and romance novels.

~Prologue~

---December 19 2003

The frantic young girl stumbled, caught herself, and continued running. Her mind was spinning. Flashes of light danced in and out of her vision. She was running for her life.

Rocks cut into her bare feet, however, she felt no pain. She could hear them behind her. Her legs pumped, carrying her forward. Trees ahead. *Just a few feet further.* Her mind screamed in fear. *Hide! Run!* She tripped, falling hard to her knees. She moved forward on all fours trying desperately to regain her footing. She pushed forward, breaking through the dense brush. Her hair caught on a branch jerking her head back. She wrenched free, feeling the strands being torn from her scalp.

Her arms moved frantically, tearing aside branches as she ran rapidly forward. A large, low hanging branch loomed in front of her. She ducked, barely escaping its spindly fingers. Pine needles crunched under her feet. *Cold.* She was so cold. She moved faster now, fear pushing her. The ground changed suddenly, sloping down. Its decline threw off her pace. Her legs were moving of their own accord now, flying forward down a steep incline, one leg in front of the other trying desperately to outdistance her upper body.

Screams from behind closer now. Losing the battle, she tumbled. Feet flying, her shoulder hit the ground hard, seconds before her body twisted. She rolled down the incline, her back slamming against the ground. Lying on a pile of pine needles, she gasped for air. She quickly rolled onto her stomach and pushed herself up on her hands and knees. Pain shot through her body. She gasped, crawling slowly, gauging her injuries. *Not so bad.*

Pain ebbing, she stood slowly. The voices were closing in. A piercing pain exploded below her shoulder blades knocking her down. Lying flat on her stomach, face in the dirt and quickly losing consciousness, she heard a triumphant yell.

"Over here! I got her!"

*Then, nothing.*

# Chapter 1

"Ten years, Danny. You've shown your dedication. Congratulations."

Danielle stared at the paper in her hand. She'd put in for the upgrade Senior Special Agent. *Wow*. Ten years on the job. She still felt young at 36, but the title made her feel more seasoned. Silly, she knew, being a woman in the field of law enforcement could be challenging. She smiled. *Every little bit helps*.

Her R.A.C. nodded, recognizing the smile. "It's good to be proud. You've earned it. Now, it's time to get back to work!" Scott Magraff had known Danielle Devon for eight years. He was the Resident Agent in Charge, or R.A.C .depending on who was doing the talking. He was the only person that ever called her Danny, much to her dismay.

In the beginning, theirs had been a love hate relationship. He, constantly trying to rein her in, she, bucking his authority every time the chance was given. It had taken some time but eventually they had gained a mutual respect.

Magraff tugged at his gray mustache. "Have you read through the details? Are you prepared?"

She nodded. "Yes sir. There are a few things I'm not clear on."

He pulled the file out of his desk and opened the cover. "It's all cut and dry. Where's the problem?"

"Well, the age thing to start. I'm going in as a 29-year-old college student. I was thinking we might want to reconsider." According to the file, she was working on her master's degree in psychology but was concerned about the seven year discrepancy in her age. In reality, Danielle Renée Devon had completed law school at the tender age of twenty-five. She had excelled in her studies, graduating in the top five of her class. Her intention had been to follow a career path toward prosecution, criminal law being her specialty. To her great surprise the FBI had recruited her soon after graduation. She quickly accepted and left for Quantico, Virginia soon after to begin her training.

Now, ten years later, she was a top agent in her field. Respected by most, hated by some. The man who faced her now across his desk fell into the first category.

He shook his head and laughed. "Have you looked in a mirror lately?" He waved his hand in the air. "Never mind. Trust me, it's not an issue. Your cover is intact. All of the documents are in place. Airline tickets, class schedule. As far as anyone knows you're chasing your dreams. Your contact in Denver is Damon Spectra, he's the SAC. Contact him as soon as you're settled. He'll set you up there."

"Are we going to have any problems with me coming in?" Danielle knew how it worked. Denver had its own. They would want to assign a lead agent out of their division. This had started out as her case and she had fought to keep it. The backlash might be bad, yet she was hoping for a smooth transition.

"There shouldn't be any. I've spoken to Spectra myself. He agrees that putting on a new lead would only slow things down. The fact that two of the missing students are from our neck of the woods makes things easier." He leaned forward, placing his hands on the desk. "This doesn't give you a free pass. Don't piss anyone off."

Her blue eyes snapped. "Give me some credit. I'll do my job. Is that all?" she asked.

His face set and serious, he regarded her. "I know you will. I expect to be kept in the loop on this. You run into any trouble, I hear about it immediately. Are we clear?"

"As a summer's day, sir." She grinned. She watched as he ran his fingers through his coarse gray hair, grabbed a pack of cigarettes, withdrew one and lit it up. Danielle was on her feet before the tip of the cigarette glowed red.

"Out," Magraff said through a puff a smoke. "Call and update ASAP."

She walked down the long row of cubicles and wondered how six young people all ended up traveling to Denver, Colorado for no apparent reason, only to disappear upon arrival. She shook her head in dismay. The deeper she delved, the weirder it seemed.

Available at your favorite book store or at:
amazon.com
barnesandnoble.com
target.com

www.a-argusbooks.com

www.ingramcontent.com/pod-product-compliance
Lightning Source LLC
Chambersburg PA
CBHW071235250626
47163CB00001B/193